THE QUEEN OF DREAMS

SECRET
THRONE

Peter F. Hamilton was born in Rutland
in 1960 and still lives in that county. He
began writing adult science fiction and
fantasy in 1987 and since then has sold
over two million books in the UK alone
and is the UK's bestselling science-
fiction author. He has two young
children who inspired him to write for
a younger audience. *The Secret Throne* is
the first book in the fantastic The Queen
of Dreams children's fantasy trilogy.

CALGARY PUBLIC LIBRARY

NOV   2015

THE QUEEN OF DREAMS

THE
SECRET
THRONE

PETER F. HAMILTON

ILLUSTRATED BY ROHAN EASON

MACMILLAN CHILDREN'S BOOKS

First published 2014 by Doubleday as *The Queen of Dreams*

This edition published 2015 by Macmillan Children's Books
an imprint of Pan Macmillan
a division of Macmillan Publishers Limited
20 New Wharf Road, London N1 9RR
Associated companies throughout the world
www.panmacmillan.com

ISBN 978-1-4472-8865-7

Text copyright © Rutland Horizon Ltd 2014
Illustrations copyright © Rohan Eason 2015

The right of Peter F. Hamilton and Rohan Eason to be identified as
the author and illustrator of this work has been asserted by them in
accordance with the Copyright, Designs and Patents Act 1988.

All rights reserved. No part of this publication may be
reproduced, stored in or introduced into a retrieval system, or
transmitted, in any form or by any means (electronic, mechanical,
photocopying, recording or otherwise), without the prior written
permission of the publisher. Any person who does any unauthorized
act in relation to this publication may be liable to criminal
prosecution and civil claims for damages.

1 3 5 7 9 8 6 4 2

A CIP catalogue record for this book is available from
the British Library.

Printed and bound by CPI Group (UK) Ltd, Croydon CR0 4YY

This book is sold subject to the condition that it shall not,
by way of trade or otherwise, be lent, resold, hired out,
or otherwise circulated without the publisher's prior consent
in any form of binding or cover other than that in which
it is published and without a similar condition including this
condition being imposed on the subsequent purchaser.

This one is for Tilly, Elsie, Rosa and Bea.

So you see girls, once upon a time Uncle Peter was actually quite cool.

CONTENTS

A HOLIDAY WITH DAD

'Just go away,' Taggie Paganuzzi whispered fiercely at the grey rain clouds that were drawing together across the bright summer sky. She and her sister were returning from a holiday with their mum to spend a fortnight with their dad. The drive had taken hours and Taggie was seriously bored.

'It's going to rain,' Jemima announced crossly. 'That's not fair. We've had lovely weather in Cornwall.'

Taggie, who was twelve, had lost count years ago of how many times every day her eleven-year-old sister said 'not fair'. It was Jemima's favourite phrase, which she gleefully applied to everything from school dinners to clothes to losing on the Wii. This time, however, Taggie was in complete agreement. Summer holidays were meant to be sunny; that was the whole reason for having them. In fact, she couldn't remember one that hadn't been warm and sunny.

The clouds were swirling and knotting together, thicker than tangles in hair. She gave them a determined stare. 'Go away,' she repeated hotly.

Sure enough, the clouds began to thin out as sharp,

unexpected flurries of wind tore at them like invisible claws. Within a minute the last wispy remnants were fleeing back to the seas where they'd come from.

'That was you,' Jemima said; her pretty heart-shaped face was tilted to one side as she regarded Taggie with a suspicious expression.

'Don't know what you mean,' Taggie replied smoothly.

'Mum!' Jemima called. 'Taggie's been cloudbusting again.'

In the driver's seat Nicola, their mother, grinned patiently. 'Has she? Well that's not a bad thing, is it?'

Jemima crossed her arms in exasperation and slumped down in her seat, which sent her sandy hair falling over her face.

Taggie glanced back out of the car, watching playful sunbeams soak into the rolling fields. She knew that what really bugged Jem was that she couldn't do it, no matter how hard she screwed up her face and yelled 'Abracadabra!' at the sky. Not that Taggie could do it every time; in fact she was mostly convinced it was all her heated imagination. But over the last few years her wistful wishes for rain to end and the sun to come out seemed to be answered favourably more often than not – which was why she used such wishes sparingly, in case anyone other than Jem noticed and realized how odd it was.

The ability had started to appear as the wonderful dreams had diminished. Taggie had never told anybody, but for every night of her first eight years she'd dreamed of a palace. It was a huge and fabulous building with tall, gold-tipped spires and grand halls and elegant apartments; and at the very heart was a huge silver and blue throne room where a Queen sat on a shell-like throne under an arching crystal roof. The Queen was a stately, graceful old lady that Taggie found imposing; with long silver hair arranged in thick waves of curls, and a wise, kind face tinged with sorrow.

Whatever suffering befell Taggie during the day – those endless squabbles with Jemima, getting woeful marks in her French exams, her hockey team being beaten 9–0, tearing a favourite dress, breaking her arm aged seven when she fell off her bicycle, Mum and Dad splitting up, Floofs the cat dying – it didn't matter how big or small the hurt, the Queen smiled sympathetically in welcome when Taggie dreamed of her. Taggie felt an overwhelming relief that someone recognized and cared about everything she was going through. It was that caring which drained away the misery, leaving her happy and full of bounce when she woke up the next morning.

But around her eighth birthday the dreams stopped coming every night, and appeared less and less often – until they were no more. Taggie really missed the quiet comfort they brought. Most nights she still fell asleep hoping the Queen would appear again. Cloudbusting seemed such a poor substitute.

They were just in time for tea when they arrived at Melham village, a few miles north of Grantham. Dad's fruit farm sat on the edge of the village, it had been in the family for generations, he told them. Once it had covered hundreds of acres, but over the centuries their land had slowly been sold off to pay debts and taxes until all that was left was Orchard Cottage, with its long paddock and ancient orchard bordering the remaining few fields.

Taggie and Jemima came hurtling out of the car. Dino Paganuzzi was waiting for them on the gravel at the end of the drive, his arms open wide.

'Daddeeeee!' they both yelled as they flung themselves on him.

He hugged his daughters. 'Hello, my darlings.'

Taggie gave him an extra squeeze. She was so pleased to see him she didn't want to let go, though she was dying to get into the cottage and start this part of the holiday. Dad grinned and went to get the cases from the car. Taggie didn't say what she was thinking, that he looked older somehow, with his hair thinning and a few more lines on his cheeks.

'Crikey, how long are you planning on staying?' he asked as he sweated and struggled with the bags and backpacks and eco-forever carriers and wicker baskets and gadget cases. 'A year?'

'Just the fortnight,' Mum said pointedly.

Taggie caught Dad giving her a sad smile as he said, 'I remember. Would you like to stay tonight? You've had a long drive.'

'No thank you,' Mum said.

4

Taggie sighed to herself. She never stopped hoping they'd get back together, even though she knew in her heart they never would. At least they were still friends.

The village of Melham was made up of dainty stone cottages and large imperious houses concealed behind high, trim hedges of yews and beech. Then there was Orchard Cottage. Its stone walls sagged and bent in odd places. And the roof was a strange combination of slate and quietly rotting thatch, mottled with bits of frayed tarpaulin Dad had tied on whenever the rain dribbled in through a new hole. Its apex bowed and curved more than a camel's back, almost as badly as the precarious chimneys.

But Taggie loved its warren of rooms and poky back stairs and beams that jutted out of walls and ceilings in unexpected places. There was no central heating and it got water from its own spring, which tasted so much better than mains water – that is, when it did eventually splutter out of the creaky brass taps. Only four rooms had electricity and they were all on the ground floor, the iron kitchen range burned coal, and there certainly wasn't any satellite TV or broadband. All of which made staying such an adventure, like camping indoors. Taggie was fully geared up for the fortnight. She'd brought her wind-up torch and lantern; her smartphone was fully charged, as was her iPad.

Once her bags were piled up on the floor of her bedroom, Taggie went downstairs to say goodbye to Mum. She got a kiss and a big hug, as did Jemima.

'Remember to phone,' Mum said as she got back into the car.

'We will,' the sisters promised.

The car wove round the overgrown rose bushes that had toppled across the gravel, and drove out past the broken gate. Taggie waved until it vanished from sight, then noticed the strange look Dad was giving her.

'You've changed your hair,' he said.

Taggie was surprised. Hairstyles weren't the kind of thing he normally noticed. Mum had treated her and Jen with a visit to an expensive hairdresser yesterday. Jen had got her hair fluffed up and frizzed, while Taggie's natural curls were finally straightened out, with two slim braids woven in to hold it off her face. She hadn't realized how long her hair actually was, though the hairdresser had warned her it would curl up again as soon as it got damp.

'Yes,' she said, delighted. 'Do you like it?'

He was looking quite puzzled now. 'You look just like . . . Sorry, that's silly of me.'

'Like who?' Taggie persisted.

'Someone I met a long time ago.'

'Mum? Everyone says I look just like her.'

'Well yes,' Dad said with an enigmatic smile. 'But the girl I'm thinking of wasn't your mother. Now come on, I've saved some strawberries from this morning's picking. Who wants some?'

'Me!' both sisters yelled excitedly.

STRANGE THINGS IN THE ORCHARD

After two helpings of strawberries, Taggie and Jemima went out into the garden to find Lightning, Dad's tortoise. Supposedly it had lived at Orchard Cottage for a hundred and eighty years, ever since a sailor ancestor brought it back from some adventurous voyage across the ocean, or so Dad claimed. They wandered round the shaggy bushes and peony trees, skirting the pond which was now mostly marsh and reeds.

'He's not here,' Jemima proclaimed as they criss-crossed the lawn for the third time. 'Let's try the orchard – he might prefer the shade.'

So they went through the kissing gate in the fuchsia hedge and into the orchard beyond. Dad always called it the fruit and nut orchard because of the amazing variety of trees planted there. The apple and pear trees were old and huge, but once upon a time they had been pruned and shaped properly, so their branches formed broad umbrellas just above the girls' heads. This year's crop was now almost ripe. Red and green apples hung like clusters of oversize grapes from the branches. Big bees were buzzing about, trying to find the last blossoms.

'Do you think we'll get to pick some?' Jemima asked as they walked through the dappled shade. The wildflowers that carpeted the ground had passed their best, with just a few flowers remaining amid the dry stalks and long grass.

'Probably,' Taggie said.

Jemima could just hear the pickers in the polytunnels on the other side of the tall hawthorn hedge, talking and laughing as they moved along the long troughs of strawberries. She was looking forward to helping with the harvest tomorrow – and earning some much needed money. Cornwall had been expensive.

There was no sign of Lightning underneath the apple trees. Then a quick flash of movement caught Jemima's eye. She moved towards it, and saw white fur, up amid the branches of the plum tree. Jemima liked cats. She hurried over and looked up, only to be surprised at the speed with which the creature zipped through the dense tangle of branches. Then her jaw dropped open in amazement as she saw it was actually a big squirrel. A white squirrel! It jumped effortlessly from one tree to the next.

'Hey!' Jemima exclaimed. One corner of the orchard had a line of hazelnut trees, and right at the end was a huge old sweet chestnut. 'You stay away from our nuts,' she scolded the squirrel. Even as she said it, she couldn't help but admire its tail; the snow-white fur was soft and fluffy enough to feature in a shampoo advert.

The squirrel turned and looked at her. That was when Jemima got the biggest shock of all. It was wearing glasses, neat little steel frames with purple lenses.

'Nobody owns nuts,' it said.

Jemima gasped. It couldn't possibly be the squirrel that had spoken. A squirrel that wore glasses! 'Hey,' she said, and started running towards it. 'Hey, was that you?'

The squirrel skipped lightly along the branch and jumped again, flying through the air with the grace of an eagle. Jemima pounded along after it, her face screwing up that way it did when she was *really* determined.

Then they were at the end of the trees and the squirrel jumped to the ground. It performed a neat forward somersault as it hit the grass, and shot off towards the hawthorn hedge.

'No way!' Jemima grunted. Just then she realized where the squirrel was heading. At the far end of the orchard was an old stone well. There was no prim little roof above, nor a chain-winding mechanism for lowering pails down to the water. This well was just a big black hole in the ground with the remnants of a fence around it. Jemima had always stayed away from it – something about that deep black hole spooked her.

The squirrel shot between the rotten posts of wood.

'Stop,' Jemima shouted. 'Be careful, that's . . .'

It was too late: the squirrel leaped on to the low rim of stone, and dived straight down the well.

Jemima squealed in horror, her hands coming up to cover her mouth. Somehow she overcame her reluctance and scrambled over the moss-covered fence. The darkness

that lurked below
the well's stone rim
was so intense it was frightening. She squirmed her way
back a bit, and listened for any sound of a struggling
squirrel.

Taggie arrived beside her, breathless and anxious. She
gave the well a nervous look and kept a couple of paces
back from the empty shaft of darkness. 'What is it? What
happened?'

'A squirrel,' Jemima cried. 'I saw a squirrel fall down
the well.' At this point she wasn't prepared to mention the
glasses. Nor the talking bit. Actually, Jemima thought it
best not to say it was white, either.

'I can't see anything . . .' Very slowly, Taggie edged
forward and squinted down the stone-lined hole.

'It's down there, I swear,' Jemima said.

'We should drop a pebble in. See how far down the
water is.'

'Hey! You two – come away from there *right* now.' It

was Dad's very cross voice. 'Come on, I mean it!'

They both turned round guiltily to see him marching through the orchard trees. He looked furious.

The sheepish sisters clambered back over the fence. One of the poles cracked sharply when Taggie put all her weight on it.

'Sorry, Daddy,' Jemima said, hanging her head. She hated it when he was cross with her. And they were only a couple of hours into the holiday.

Dad put an arm round each girl's shoulder, and steered them away from the fence. 'It's all right. It's partly my fault. I should never have let the fence get so dilapidated. I'll fix it properly tomorrow.' He glanced back over his shoulder with a worried expression.

'Maybe close it permanently . . .' he muttered to himself. 'I still have the entitlement to do that. Yes I do. That cannot be taken from me.'

'But . . . Daddy, I saw a squirrel fall down it,' Jemima insisted.

Dad stopped. 'What sort of squirrel?'

Which Jemima thought was a strange kind of question for him to ask. 'Just a squirrel,' she said, trying not to sound too guilty.

'It'll be fine,' Dad assured them. 'Squirrels are the best climbers. It was probably scared of you two waiting at the top.'

'How deep is the well?' Jemima asked. 'It's very dark.'

'Deep enough to need a fence round it,' Dad said. 'It's

very dangerous. So I want both of you to promise me you'll stay away.'

'Yes, Dad,' they mumbled.

'Oh the enthusiasm, it's overwhelming. Will you please stay away?'

'YES, DAD.'

'Better.' He hugged them both. 'Much better. Now come on, let's see if we can find Lightning. He's been eating my lettuces this year, the rotten thing. We'll start in the vegetable patch.'

3

SECRETS IN THE NIGHT

Taggie didn't hear the footsteps outside her room after she was supposed to be asleep, nor did she see the lantern-light shining through the gap at the bottom of her door. She didn't hear the door handle creak open because her earphones were set at full volume – which Mum always told her not to do, claiming she'd be deaf before she was twenty.

The door swung open, and the figure framed by the light gawped in surprise at Taggie, who, dressed in her loose jim-jams, was bending backwards as she aimed a solid kick at the head of a target mannequin. The somewhat unrealistic figure had been made from a mop, various sticks, and some of Dad's old clothes, found in another bedroom.

Taggie's foot missed the bristling grey head and she nearly lost her balance as she stared at the equally surprised Jemima standing in the doorway. She hurriedly turned the music off.

'What are you doing?' Jemima asked.

'Practising,' Taggie said impatiently. 'I didn't do any in Cornwall. My sensei, Mr Koimosi, said it's very important to keep fresh.'

It was six months now since Taggie had swapped ballet for the much more exciting kick-boxing class at the local gym. Mum had grumbled about how unladylike it was, but signed the forms anyway. Taggie hadn't *quite* got round to telling Dad yet.

She pulled Jemima inside quickly and shut the door.

'You haven't told Dad yet, have you?' Jemima said shrewdly.

'You know what he's like. He wouldn't let you play rugby.'

Jemima's lips curled up victoriously, an expression Taggie was dangerously familiar with. 'And if you ever tell him, I'll say who left the gate open the day Harrod escaped.'

'I didn't!'

Taggie took her earphones out. 'I saw you. You went out on your bike and forgot to close it after.'

'Oh. And you never told?'

'No.' Taggie paused just long enough. 'Not yet.'

'Thank you,' Jemima said meekly. It had taken six hours to find the neighbour's Labrador puppy that day.

'What do you want, Jem?'

'I saw something,' Jemima said in a whisper. 'Something in the garden. I couldn't sleep, I'm not tired, so I was looking out of the window. The news said there's supposed to be meteors tonight.'

'What did you see?'

'I don't know. It's quite dark out there. Whatever it

was, it was slinking round the fuchsia hedge.'

Taggie suddenly felt cold. She glanced nervously at her bedroom window. 'A burglar?'

'I don't know. It was all black. Like a shadow that wasn't attached to anything.'

'All right, hang on.' Taggie switched off her lantern. Jemima flicked hers off, too. Slowly Taggie pulled the curtains back, fearful that any sharp movement would pull the rickety old curtain pole off the wall. The sisters leaned on the windowsill and peered out into the garden.

Hundreds of stars twinkled in a cloudless sky; their thin, silky light illuminated a dark lawn surrounded by black bushes. Taggie watched for several minutes. 'There's nothing out there, Jem,' she said. Once again she was playing the big sister role, being all positive and reassuring.

'Taggie, please,' Jemima pleaded. 'I saw something. And . . .' She took a big breath, screwing up her courage. 'Don't laugh, but there was something really odd about that squirrel this afternoon.'

'What sort of odd?'

'It was white.'

'Really?'

'Yes. I swear. And, it was wearing glasses, and—'

'Glasses?' Taggie interrupted with a sceptical stare.

'I knew you'd laugh,' whined Jemima.

'I'm not laughing.'

'You saw how Dad behaved at the well this afternoon.

He was more scared than he was angry. There's something odd going on, Taggie.'

Taggie pulled the curtains closed again and switched her lantern back on. She remembered very clearly Dad asking: *What sort of squirrel?* 'All right, let's go and tell him something's out there.'

'No!' Jemima implored. She pulled at Taggie's arm.

'He's our dad, Jem. He won't want us upset over something that might or might not be lurking outside.'

'Well . . . you say *you* saw it, then.'

Taggie sighed. Sometimes being the big sister could be such an effort. 'All right. Come on.'

They heard people talking as they reached the bottom of the stairs, where there were some electric lights. At first Taggie thought Dad must have the TV on loud. Then she remembered he didn't have a TV. Dad liked books: two rooms downstairs had floor-to-ceiling shelving completely filled with books, and there were piles and piles on every piece of furniture too.

The radio, then, Taggie told herself as they approached the lounge door. But one of the voices was Dad's.

'I will not return,' he was saying insistently.

'But, sire, the situation is most grave.'

Taggie frowned, the person Dad was talking to had a strange gurgly sort of voice, as if there was liquid bubbling through his throat as he spoke.

'I have other responsibilities now,' Dad said.

'What could possibly be more important?'

'I do not wish to discuss this . . .'

Taggie stepped on a loose floorboard, which creaked loudly. She recovered fast; holding Jemima's hand, she walked forward as if nothing was wrong.

The lounge door was flung open. 'What are you two doing down here?' Dad demanded. He wasn't angry; more like anxious.

'I thought I saw something,' Taggie said. 'I couldn't get to sleep, so I was looking out of the window for shooting stars. Then something moved in the garden.'

'I saw it too,' Jemima piped up. She was squeezing Taggie's hand hard.

'What?' Dad asked. 'What was outside?'

'Don't know – it was big and dark,' Jemima blurted. 'Is it a burglar, Daddy?'

Dad put his arms round her. 'Oh my darling . . . No of course not. We don't get burglars out here. Besides, there's nothing worth stealing in this old place.'

Taggie was staring into the

lounge. A couple of dim wall lights acted more like candles than electric bulbs, casting deep shadows across the room. Even in the gloom there was a strange shadow that she was drawn to; it was almost like a mist flowing around Dad's antique wingback chair. Her eyes couldn't quite focus properly, and it wasn't black like an ordinary shadow, but the darkest red instead. She blinked and squinted hard, concentrating on the weird mirage. The shadow abruptly came into focus as an elderly man in long flowing robes. Taggie thought her eyes were still acting oddly: his skin looked as red as an earthenware pot.

'Sorry for interrupting,' she said to him. 'We didn't know Dad had a visitor.'

The man's whole body jumped as if she'd poked him with a stick rather than just said a polite greeting. He gave her a shocked stare.

'What?' her dad blurted, he looked from Taggie to the man. 'You can see . . . ?'

'Who are you talking to?' Jemima asked.

As if a whole new set of lights had been switched on, the man in the chair abruptly came into sharp focus.

'Oh!' a startled Jemima blurted. 'Sorry, I didn't see you there.'

'Ah . . . Right . . .' Dad stammered. 'Girls, this is Mr Anatole, he's the . . . er, new village vicar. He's here to discuss the church fete.'

'Delighted to meet you.' Mr Anatole rose from the seat. He was at least a head taller than Dad, and his robes were like nothing Taggie had ever seen before. The cloth was a rich heavy mix of scarlet, indigo and emerald, with elaborate patterns in gold thread. It was something a bishop might wear, not a rural vicar. And he would have to be a very important bishop, Taggie decided.

'What's happened to your skin?' Jemima asked.

'Jem!' Taggie hissed, furious with her sister for being so rude.

'Jemima!' Dad snapped crossly.

Jemima hung her head, hair curtaining down across her eyes. 'Sorry.'

'That's quite all right,' Mr Anatole said. 'Dear girl, I've had this skin since I was born.'

'Oh, I see,' an abashed Jemima muttered.

'Now look,' Dad said in a kindly voice. 'It's very late. You two are supposed to be asleep. I understand you're worried, so . . . This is the deal, you go back to bed, and I'll take a look round the garden when Mr Anatole leaves – which is going to be very soon, OK? Now go on upstairs.' He kissed both of them. 'Go on.'

'Night, Dad,' they chorused.

'Goodnight, Mr Anatole,' Taggie added.

The lounge door shut. Taggie was halfway back up the stairs when she heard Mr Anatole saying: 'Sire, you have daughters!'

'Be silent,' Dad snapped coldly.

Taggie couldn't remember him being so sharp with anyone before, let alone a vicar. She and Jemima ran all the way back to their bedrooms. With the door closed and the lantern off, Taggie burrowed under her duvet, as if that would shield her from all the strange events of the day. Sleep came surprisingly quickly, but though she was really hoping the Queen would be there to comfort her, it was not to be.

4

STRAWBERRIES AND KIDNAPPING

After they woke up, Taggie and Jemima were sent out to collect eggs from the hen-coop, which took up a quarter of the kitchen garden. Then Dad cooked them breakfast on the big iron range, spending half his time poking at the glowing coals through the grate. 'It gets the air flowing,' he explained sheepishly as a small avalanche of ash slipped out on to the red tile floor.

They had poached eggs with thick rashers of bacon, and big fried tomatoes which Dad had grown at the end of a polytunnel. It was accompanied by slices of freshly baked bread and honey. Taggie didn't think she'd be able to move afterwards, she'd eaten so much.

'Time to start picking,' Dad announced.

Groaning, Taggie and Jemima followed him to the fields where the polytunnels were set up. For someone who seemed to enjoy living life from about two centuries ago, Dad had certainly adapted to modern fruit growing. Each polytunnel had five long troughs of strawberry plants running the entire length. Stems with huge bunches of ripe, scarlet strawberries hung over the edges, at a perfect height for picking.

Several pickers lived in caravans that were parked at the bottom of the field; they were traditional Romanies who visited each year. Some of the families claimed their ancestors had been coming since Orchard Cottage was first built. As they walked to work they were joined by more pickers from the village and nearby town who rode up on bicycles and scooters.

Dad's old tractor puttered about, delivering pallets of empty boxes to the end of each row, and the pickers started to collect the fruit. The strawberries had all been contracted to a specialist supplier who dealt in organic fruit. Dad might have adopted polytunnels and irrigation pipes, but he hated the idea of using chemicals of any kind. 'Nature knows best,' he always told the girls.

Taggie believed him. She started off eating plenty of strawberries as she picked them. They tasted utterly delicious, so much better than anything from the supermarkets.

'What did you think of that man last night?' Jem asked when they were by themselves, halfway along the polytunnel.

'I've never seen clothes like that,' Taggie admitted.

'He's not from here,' Jemima said.

'Dad said he's the vicar.'

'He's not.'

'Are you calling Dad a liar?' snapped Taggie.

Jemima pursed her lips. 'He's from a long way away, and that's that.'

'Don't be ridiculous,' said Taggie. 'You don't know anything about him.'

'I do! I know he's not from here.'

'How do you know?'

'I always know things like that.'

'Now you're just being stupid.'

'You're just jealous cos I'm smarter than you.'

'You are not,' Taggie growled.

'Am too.' Jemima picked up her tray and stomped off down the polytunnel.

Taggie nearly shouted after her, but reminded herself that she was the older sister, and such things didn't bother her at all. So there. She went back to picking.

A lot of the strawberries were still pale green, so Taggie had to check to make sure she only picked the ripe ones. It was monotonous work, and the air trapped in the polytunnel was stifling. She was certainly earning her money.

Halfway through the morning she realized people were singing in the next polytunnel. When she looked up she saw her polytunnel was nearly deserted. Taggie wandered out, intrigued by the laughter coming from the other polytunnel where Jem had gone.

When she looked round the edge, she saw nearly every picker was moving along the raised troughs. And no wonder they were all happy and smiling. The strawberries were all a rich scarlet. Every one of them had ripened. She saw Jemima halfway down the polytunnel, her face smeared red from berry juice, and grinning from ear to ear as she threw berries into her tray.

'It's because I sent the clouds away,' Taggie told herself. 'The sun must have ripened them all at once.'

In only one polytunnel? a small voice in her head asked. Taggie sighed and went back to her own picking.

That afternoon, both Taggie and Jemima ducked out of work. Dad was in the old barn, sawing up lengths of planks to use as fencing around the well. They helped him carry the heavy wood across the lawn and through the kissing gate in the fuchsia hedge. Taggie looked round the orchard in amazement. The wildflowers under the trees, which yesterday had been faded and dying back, had returned in full bloom. The whole orchard was ablaze with colour. Bees were flitting excitedly between the flowers, emitting a low droning sound.

'That's better,' Jemima said contentedly.

Dad started pulling down what was left of the old fence. Taggie took the rotten wood back into the garden and dumped it all in the bonfire pit.

'No good for the log stove in the cottage,' Dad said. 'It's too damp, but it'll do fine for a bonfire in autumn.'

After that it got a bit boring. Dad was using a fencing spade to dig new holes for the corner posts, which was hard work. The sisters tried using it, but the ground was tough and full of small stones, which had to be prised out individually.

Taggie made some tea, which she and Jemima had on the patio while Dad carried on digging. Just as they were finishing, they heard a commotion coming from the orchard; some loud *thuds*, then the sound of metal striking metal.

'What on earth is Dad doing now?' Taggie wondered. They headed towards the kissing gate. Just before they reached it they heard Dad cry out – a wordless shout of rage followed by another almighty *clang*.

Taggie and Jemima looked at each other, then dashed for the gate.

They sprinted into the orchard, scattering lazy bees out of the way. Dad was at the top of the well holding a spade like a cricket bat, swinging at some creatures around him. There were three of them, no higher than his waist, dressed in shiny armour the lurid colour of blood. At first Taggie thought they were dwarfs, but then she saw they had four legs apiece. What could be seen through the helmet visors was a vague impression of hairy faces and noses like pigs' snouts. The strange creatures lunged and stabbed at Dad with short swords. He fended them off with equally skilful jabs and swipes with his sturdy fencing spade. As the girls ran closer he unleashed a flurry of blows, dinting the knights' already battered shields. One of them fell to the ground as Dad caught it a good blow on the side of its head.

Then two more popped up out of the well. They flung a silvery net, which twisted round Dad's arm

before wrapping itself around his legs.

'No!' Taggie screamed, and dashed forward.

Dad turned in shock. 'Stay away,' he bellowed.

Taggie stopped, even though she was desperate to run over to him. To help somehow.

'Go to your mother,' Dad yelled. 'Tell her what's happened.'

Taggie saw one of the four-legged knight-things hit Dad with a thick wooden baton across the back of his legs, forcing him down on to his knees. Another net was thrown, covering him completely this time. But he still had the spade, which he jabbed at the little armoured figures.

'Do not follow me,' he roared at his daughters. 'Run! Run away *now*. Get to your mother! You'll be safe with—' Another wooden baton smacked into him.

'Daddeeeee!' Taggie shrieked in horror. Beside her, Jemima was screaming in panic.

Taggie's voice abruptly died in her throat. Something was sliding up smoothly from the centre of the well: a figure dressed in a long black cloak that swirled as if it was made from thick smoke. His face was just visible deep inside the baggy hood, like a skull with a thin layer of skin the colour of a white slug. He wore wide wrap-around sunglasses perched on a flat, thin nose with a single nostril. And when the narrow lips opened to sneer at her unsuspecting father's back, she saw silver teeth ending in sharp points.

Taggie cried out in horror. The man-creature reached out with fingers twice as long as a human's and covered in a gaudy collection of silver and crystal rings. Those gruesome hands closed over her father's shoulders, and pulled him backwards.

'Go! Get away!' Dad shouted desperately. Then he was gone, pulled down into the darkness with the man-creature. The horrid little knight-things jumped down after them.

Taggie ran forward, despite everything her father had

yelled at her. Determination burned like fire beneath her skin. Her *dad* had been kidnapped – it didn't matter by what. One of the red-armoured knights was still on the rim of the well, wobbling about as it adjusted its helmet. She was going to grab a fence post – oh yes she was – and give it a beating that would reduce it to a sobbing mess; then she'd . . .

Something white and fluffy, the size of a beach ball but not nearly as soft, slammed into her side and sent her sprawling painfully across the grass.

'Huh?' she wheezed.

'You heard your father,' a voice said in her ear. 'Do not challenge the Rannalal knights and their Karrak master. Not here, not now.'

'The *what*?'

'You!' Jemima yelled as she ran over to her sister.

Taggie struggled to sit up. A very big white squirrel was standing in front of her, a paw pushing purple-lensed glasses back up its nose. Although the sight was astounding, she tried to peer round it. Over by the well, the remaining Rannalal knight lifted its visor to stare at her with eyes that were black balls with tiny sparks of violet in the centre. Taggie hesitated as it sneered at her, exposing long dirty fangs.

'You wish to come with us too?' it snarled in a deep voice. 'You wish to challenge me?' The short sword was raised. It took a step forward.

Taggie and Jemima yelped in fright.

'*Degot thok,*' the squirrel said loudly; he waved his front paws about. '*Metrow metrow.*'

Every bee in the orchard took off in an explosion of harsh buzzing, and zoomed towards the Rannalal knight, forming a fast, noisy, airborne river. The four-legged creature gave a startled gasp and slammed its visor down. The first wave of bees bashed into the blood-red armour, sounding like hailstones hitting a greenhouse roof. Frantic shouts echoed over the orchard as the knight slashed its sword around madly, attempting to beat the bees off while trying desperately to keep its balance. Still more bees arrived, clotting the air around the mad dancing figure. All of a sudden, it turned and jumped into the well.

The thick cloud of bees spread out, and started buzzing back to the wildflowers.

'*Gorek maw,*' the squirrel said, nodding formally at the dispersing cloud of bees.

'What?' Jemima asked.

'It means *thank you,*' Taggie said, then frowned in puzzlement at how she understood the strange language.

'In hivetalk, yes,' the squirrel confirmed.

'Who on Earth are you?' Taggie blurted, still too shocked by everything to think straight.

'The name's Felix, ma'am,' the squirrel said, bowing low at the sisters. 'I'm a special agent of the First Realm's royal palace guard.'

5

WHO YOU REALLY ARE

'Royal palace guard?' Taggie asked for what must have been the fifth time. They were back in the kitchen. Jemima had found the first-aid box for Taggie's grazed knees. When she opened it, all they found was a dried-up tube of antiseptic ointment and three small plasters. Jemima shut it again with a sigh.

'That's right,' Felix said, with pride in his voice.

'But you're a squirrel.' It was as if Taggie's mind had finally started to acknowledge all the strangeness of the last day.

The tip of Felix's tail curled down, as if it was wilting. 'For each day outside my birthday and while the snow falls on oak,' he said with a sad voice. 'I am from the First Realm.'

'What's that?' Jemima asked.

Felix looked from Jemima to Taggie. 'Has your father not spoken of this to you?'

'No,' Taggie said, narrowing her eyes.

'Oh dear.' Felix's tail swished about in agitation. 'I never thought I'd be the one having to explain this. You see, your father was born in the First Realm.'

31

'What is the First Realm?' Jemima asked again.

'The world beyond this one; you might call it the land of Faerie.'

'That sounds just like a story,' Jemima protested.

'A talking squirrel just told you that,' Taggie said gruffly. 'Think about it.'

Jem shot her a venomous look.

'Stories drift across from the First Realm and secure themselves in your legends,' Felix said; his shiny black eyes regarded Jemima kindly. 'Those of us who have permission to cross through either bring such tales or have them told about us. Such crossings are rare in these days; this Outer Realm is not pleasant to our kind any more.'

'Then why would Dad come here from this . . . er, First Realm you keep talking about?' Taggie asked.

'He was very young when he left his destiny and obligations behind on a quest to find a girl. Like most young men of his upbringing, he was a romantic.'

'He must have come to find Mum,' Jemima said delightedly. 'How wonderful!'

Felix flexed his front paws. 'Is your mother here?' he asked hopefully.

'Er, no. They separated five years ago. We're just staying with Dad for the holidays,' replied Jemima.

'I can't believe he never told us any of this,' Taggie muttered. Now the shock and worry was fading, she was getting really quite cross with Dad.

'The knowledge of your heritage is a burden for

anyone so young,' Felix said.

Jemima's face had a rapturous expression. 'Hang on. You said you're in the *royal* palace guard?'

Felix's paws moved fast, as if he was scrabbling at something. 'Yes?' he agreed cautiously.

'Why are you here? Is it to protect Dad?'

'Yes. Prince Dino was remarkably hard to find. No one ever dared guess he had crossed to *this* realm.'

'A prince! Dad's a prince,' Jemima said with a cry. 'And I'm his daughter. That means I'm royalty!'

Taggie rolled her eyes and groaned in dismay at her sister's behaviour.

'They'll all have to bow and curtsy to me at school,' Jemima went on. 'And we'll go to parties in London, like those ones in Mum's *Hello!* magazine. Oh Taggie, we'll be celebrities.'

Taggie hadn't taken her eyes off Felix, whose fur was rising the way cats did when they were unsettled. 'I don't think it works like that, Jem,' she said levelly. 'Felix, there was a strange man called Mr Anatole here last night. He had red skin and he was hard to see. He and Dad were talking. Who is he?'

Felix's teeth chittered together as if he was chewing an invisible nut. 'Mr Anatole was the equerry, or adviser, to your late, esteemed grandmother. Like me, he only found out where your father was living a few days ago.'

'He wanted Dad to go back, didn't he? Back to your First Realm.'

'Yes,' Felix said. 'Mr Anatole is a Shadarain. Although not a fully schooled mage, he is—'

'A mage? That's like wizard, isn't it?' asked Taggie.

'Similar, yes. Mr Anatole is schooled in magic,' said Felix hesitantly. 'And a renowned shadecaster, which helps him move around unseen. All the better to gather knowledge, and advise your grandmother's court.'

'Grandmother?' Jemima squeaked. 'We have a grandma?'

'I'm afraid not,' Felix said sadly. 'She passed away several years ago. Which is why the First Realm needs your father.' His voice dropped. 'And now you.'

'*Us?*' Taggie said in surprise. 'That can't be right? Who were those four-legged . . . *things* in red armour, and that terrible man-creature in a cloak? Why did they kidnap Dad?'

Felix clasped his front paws together. 'The four-legged knights are called the Rannalal, who are loyal only to the largest, shiniest coin. The other person was a Karrak Lord, Lord Golzoth, in fact – a member of the most fierce and powerful force of darkness and ruin in all the realms.

They came to capture your father because everyone thinks he is the sole heir to the shell throne of the First Realm. You see, your grandmother was the Queen of Dreams . . .' Felix's voice softened. 'She comforted all of us who dwell in the First Realm. Every night she showed us kindness and wisdom and such dazzling compassion. We thanked her even as we dreaded the day when she would finally pass away, for we knew few are capable of such selfless spirit. It was her generosity and pure heart which held us together as a happy people and made each day worth living. She ruled the sky for us and loved us as much as we loved her.'

'And she lived in a palace,' Taggie whispered. 'With a silver and blue throne room which has a roof of crystal.'

Felix's tail fluffed up. '*Yes*. How did you know?'

Jemima was giving her sister a *very* strange look. 'Yes, Taggie. How *did* you know that?'

Taggie ignored her. 'But she died, you say?' she asked the white squirrel.

'Indeed, Princess. Now she is gone, the Karrak Lord, Jothran, who calls himself the *King of Night*, has risen and seeks to steal her throne. Life in the First Realm has become haunted and dark since he and his Karrak brethren appeared. Their fear spreads across the land like poison. It was his corrupted seers who sent spies out to this realm to find your father. I followed them, as did Mr Anatole. Alas, I am not strong enough to fight off a whole squad of Rannalal knights, let alone Lord Golzoth.'

Taggie did her best to ignore Felix calling her

'Princess' – though it was kind of pleasing. 'So Lord Golzoth is the Karrak Lord who took Dad?'

'Yes, ma'am. Lord Golzoth is second only to the King of Night when it comes to evil and treachery. He is Jothran's brother and chief enforcer.'

'What does he want with Dad?' Taggie asked. 'Dad said he didn't want to go back – I heard him tell Mr Anatole that.'

Felix's white tail swept from side to side. 'It is your father's blood which is so valuable to the King of Night. The Karrak Lords seek to end your family's line and establish their own. The King of Night didn't know that the two of you existed. But now I fear he will, and you are in grave danger.'

'Do you mean they're going to kill Dad?' Taggie yelled.

Jemima's hands had clamped over her mouth. 'Daddy,' she whimpered.

'I'm sorry,' Felix said, and lowered his head, paws covering his pointy ears. 'But I will protect *you*, my life is sworn to that task.'

Taggie leaned forward in her chair and put her face inches from Felix's little nose – just to make sure he fully understood. 'I'm glad you've dedicated yourself to protecting me. I expect I'll need all the help I can get to rescue Dad from the Karrak Lords.'

'But ma'am . . . the danger . . .' Felix spluttered.

'If I am a royal of the First Realm, that makes you my subject, so you have to do as I order you, right?'

Felix's teeth chittered again. 'That's not how . . . Your grandmother would never boss people around in such a fashion. It is not how royalty behaves.'

'OK. Then you stay here with Jem. Make sure she's safe.'

'I'm not staying here,' Jemima exclaimed heatedly.

'Yes, you *are*.'

Jemima was perfectly still for a moment as she put on her most belligerent expression. Then very slowly she took her mobile out of her jeans pocket and held it up. 'Want to let Mum decide?' she challenged.

'Ha! You wouldn't . . .'

Jemima flicked the menu round to the speed-dial list. 'The last thing Dad said was to get her.'

'Oh, for goodness sake!' Taggie snapped. 'All right, you can come too. But you have to do as I tell you.'

A triumphant Jemima switched her mobile back off again.

'No, no, no!' said Felix; his tail bashed the floor several times in agitation. 'Please, I beg you both to reconsider.'

The sisters looked at him. 'Not a chance,' they chorused.

6

HEIRLOOMS AND THE ROUNDADOWN

It was dark by the time Taggie, Jemima and Felix left Orchard Cottage. There had been a surprising amount of preparation. Felix told them how the First Realm was now cold and dark: 'The King of Night has ruined the sky. Now the cold rain has become snow, and where once sunbeams danced all day there is only a grim flicker of light.'

Taggie dressed herself in black jeans and a long-sleeve top underneath her purple and orange sweater. She shoved her feet into ankle-length boots, and carried a quilted orange coat. Once she was ready, she started filling her coat pockets with anything useful she could find: the wind-up torch of course, and a penknife that Dad had given her years ago – one with lots of blades and things. That was when she heard a sound coming from Dad's room – a heavy knocking, as if someone was desperate to be let in. Then there was the sound of something crashing on to the floor. She and Jemima rushed out into the corridor to see the squirrel standing in front of her father's room, a lantern dangling from his paw.

'Wait, Princess,' Felix said as Taggie turned the door

handle. 'This is what I'm trained for.' He settled his glasses on his face, then carefully poked his head round the door. 'There is no danger here,' he said, and opened the door wide.

His definition of 'no danger' was clearly a little different to Taggie's. The big old oak chest of drawers where Dad kept half of his clothes was rocking from side to side, as if attempting to dance. It subsided as Taggie and Jemima edged in. The third drawer shot open. There was a small ornate box inside. Taggie stepped forward and opened it. There were two things inside: some kind of bracelet, and a small suede pouch. Each had an envelope beside them, one addressed to Taggie, the other to Jemima.

Taggie opened hers, it read:

My darling Taggie,
If for any reason I have to go away, I want you to have this charm bracelet.
  It has been in our family for generations, and can be used to bring the wearer luck, among other things.
Know that I always love you,
Daddy xxx

'Oh,' Taggie gulped. Her eyes had suddenly filled with tears. The bracelet was made from several engraved bands of brass and wood which had been twisted together. As she held it up for closer examination it somehow slipped down her hand and on to her wrist. Before her eyes it shrank to a perfect fit. There was no way she could slip it back off again.

'What is it?' she asked in wonder. The bands were all turning, making a soft sound, like well-oiled machinery, as if someone was turning a combination lock. They stopped moving abruptly. Taggie could finally focus on the engravings, small symbols of which she only recognized a few: those for water, stone, cloud, waves, sun, star, flower. Then there were simple shapes: triangle, square, cone, pentagon, the sign for infinity . . . It looked Egyptian to her.

'Why, it's one of the First Realm's crown jewels,' whispered Felix. 'I didn't know it was missing. Prince Dino must have taken it with him when he left.'

Jemima opened her envelope.

My darling Jemima,
If for any reason I have to go away, I want you to
have the purse and everything it holds.
    Spend it wisely, though when you are old enough
a trip to Mrs Veroomes wouldn't hurt.
I love you dearly,
Daddy xxx

The contents of the suede purse spilt out into Jemima's palm. She blinked in delight at the pile of heavy gold coins glinting in the light of the lantern, as bright as they day they'd been minted. Her forefinger poked through them, and she frowned slightly at the four worn dice lurking there. They were so dark and old she could barely make out the symbols. She ignored them, and admired the coins again.

'Oh wow,' she gasped. 'Is this worth much?'

Felix's little wet nose twitched. 'In the First Realm that many gold coins would buy you food, clothes, drink and a duke's lodging for five years. And you'd still have some left over for parties every night.'

'Way to go, Dad,' Jemima murmured. 'But I'm going to give it all back when we rescue you.' She tipped the coins and dice back into the purse.

'I think we're as ready as we're ever going to be,' Taggie said. Now they were about to set off she was suddenly apprehensive. *Best not think about it then*, she told herself.

Jemima had also selected warm clothes and a navy blue waterproof coat, topping off with her red, white and blue-striped bobble hat, which she pulled down tight over her frizzy hair when they got to the kitchen door. Felix opened it, and peered out into the night. The garden was very dark. Clouds covered the stars. Jemima turned to frown at Felix. 'How can you see anything in those glasses at night?' she asked.

His whiskers quivered. 'These are magic spy glasses,' he explained. 'I always wear them in this Realm.'

'Really? Do they shoot laser beams, or something?' Jemima asked.

'No,' Felix said wearily. 'I bought them from an anamage in the Second Realm.'

'The Second Realm?' Taggie asked in surprise. 'Just how many Realms are there?'

'Twelve *main* ones,' Felix said. 'Though there is not much travel to the Eleventh and Twelfth.'

'Twelve!' Jemima squeaked.

'Yes. All with their own peoples and cultures. The Second Realm is the home of the anamages—'

'Are anamages wizards, like Mr Anatole?' interrupted Taggie.

'Not quite,' said Felix with a sigh. 'And I did explain that Mr Anatole is a *mage*, not a wizard. The magic of the anamages is different, it uses contraptions and devices to work. These glasses let me *see* magic. People from the other realms have a glow around them – and spells and charms shine like fireflies. It's extremely useful.'

Taggie switched on her torch as they crossed the lawn, heading for the kissing gate. Jemima's beam waved about next to hers.

'What exactly is at the bottom of the well?' Taggie asked in a whisper.

'It is called a roundadown,' Felix said.

'What's one of them, then?' Jemima asked in a loud voice.

'A roundadown is a path which leads down. *Obviously*,' said Felix.

'To what?'

'This one leads to Arasath, one of the Great Gateways between the Realms.'

'The gateways have names?' Taggie asked as they went through the kissing gate.

'The Great Gateways carry the name of the mages of the Universal Fellowship who created them. They are magical, which is why they know if you have been granted the right to cross over into the Outer Realm.'

'Do we have that right?' Taggie asked worriedly.

'It is your family, among others, which grants people the right to travel to the First Realm. Arasath will open for you. In fact, it is said that Arasath—' He stopped suddenly, and peered forward. 'Oh no.'

'What?' Jemima asked.

Felix's paw closed round Jemima's hand, forcing her to shine the torch beam through the orchard trees. It found the figure of a garden gnome wearing a long pointed hat, a blue waistcoat and orange trousers.

Taggie might have thought it cute if she hadn't seen the mean expression on his face, which was made worse by a wide open mouth revealing nasty sharp fangs.

'Eeuw,' Jemima grunted. 'I thought garden gnomes were supposed to be nice!'

'I didn't even know Dad had gnomes,' Taggie muttered. She certainly didn't remember seeing it in the orchard before; and Jem was right, this one was quite peculiar. Its arms were raised as if in anger.

'I see another out there!' Felix called out, his paw pointing.

Taggie swung her torch beam round. It swept across another gnome, this one in a green coat. And it looked as if it was moving towards them. 'Huh?' Taggie gulped. A gnome, *moving*? She brought the torch beam back carefully to where the gnome had been. It was now locked in a running posture, but closer to them.

'That was odd,' Taggie grunted. 'I could've sworn I saw it—'

A hot pain jabbed up her leg and she screamed. She brought the torch beam down and stared in horror. Right behind her was another gnome in a red jacket and green trousers, one arm extended, holding a small dagger which had stabbed through her jeans and into her calf. Blood was seeping out through the denim.

7

THE GREAT GATEWAY

Taggie kicked her leg forward, away from the blade, and the gnome fell over on its face, still fixed in its stabbing position.

'Keep the light on it,' Felix yelled as Taggie tried to look at her wound. 'They can't move in bright light.'

Jemima hurriedly waved her torch back to where she'd been shining it on the first gnome. Now it was several metres closer, frozen in a running crouch with a malicious snarl on its face.

'Hold the beam steady,' Felix warned her.

'They're alive!' Taggie exclaimed breathlessly. She couldn't see the second gnome her beam had illuminated. Fright made her keep the torch shining on the one that had stabbed her.

'They're nasty little beasts,' Felix whispered. 'They allied themselves with the Karrak Lords . . . Now keep the torches on them at all times, and walk with me towards the roundadown. Quickly now, I'm guessing there'll be more than three.'

'So did Arasath let them through as well?' Taggie asked as they carefully walked backwards, with Felix's paw guiding her.

Felix cocked his head to one side, pointed ears flicking about. 'It *must* have. But it is most strange. Nobody really likes gnomes.' The beam wasn't particularly strong, and Jemima could see the two gnomes getting dimmer behind them. Then suddenly they were gone. She squealed in fright. They'd moved so fast.

'There!' Felix shouted. He helped her slide the torch beam round. It flashed across one of the gnomes, not ten metres away now. Frozen with one foot in the air.

'Where's the other one?' Jemima yelled. Too late she heard the rush of small feet. Felix kicked savagely into the darkness outside the two torch beams. There was a grunt of pain as the gnome tumbled backwards. Taggie's beam swept across the creature, locking it into a pinwheel shape as it flew through the air. Then Felix drew a sword. Taggie had no time to wonder where he'd been concealing it before the blade shone with a sleek, green light. She was swinging the torch beam round from side to side, frantically trying to find a gnome. Felix slashed with the sword, there was a *clang*, and a tiny dagger dropped out of the air.

'My lantern's in my bag!' Taggie suddenly remembered.

'Get it!' Felix exclaimed.

Taggie let her torch drop as she fumbled for the small backpack she was carrying. Felix and Jemima stood back to back, Jemima sweeping her torch around, Felix holding the sword ready in front of him. Jemima's beam found a gnome in the middle of a leap, and it toppled to the ground, motionless. She kept the beam on it. Shapes were moving through the gloom of the orchard now. Too many shapes, Taggie saw, as she struggled with the flap on the top of her bag.

'Hurry!' Felix shouted.

Taggie saw the symbols on her bracelet starting to glow with a thin orange light. Strange memories began to race through her mind, as blurred as any recollection of a dream. Then her hand closed round the lantern in her bag, and she tugged it out, holding it high. Her thumb hit the switch.

A wide pool of bright white light splashed out. Seven gnomes were caught in its radiance, instantly becoming

still. They formed a loose circle around the trio, arms raised as they held up various nasty weapons, legs petrified in mid-stride. The lantern's light had immobilized their faces in scowls of hatred.

Jemima let out a sob of relief.

'Let's go,' Felix said quietly.

'Are there any more?' Taggie asked.

'I can see a couple,' Felix admitted. 'But they're staying well outside the light. Ma'am, please, we need to go.'

Still holding the lantern up high, Taggie stepped carefully through the wildflowers. Her leg was hurting quite badly now, and she winced at every step. Shadows of the tree trunks flowed slowly across the ground as she moved. Her heart beat faster as she realized she was carrying the light away from the circle of gnomes. 'They'll start moving again,' she exclaimed.

'Yes,' Felix said. His paw was gripping Jemima's hand tight now, helping the frightened girl along. 'But they can't get close enough to harm us.'

'OK.' Taggie nodded fearfully, and kept walking. She had to pass between two stationary gnomes, which was awful, but she kept going. Then she couldn't help but grimace as the edge of the light left two gnomes behind. Jemima shone her torch where they'd been, but she wasn't quick enough, the gnomes were free. The sound of tiny running feet came at them like a breeze through the darkness. Just a few paces later, all the gnomes that'd been caught in the lantern's light were in darkness. It seemed as if they were surrounded by the sound of them slithering through the grass.

After what seemed an age, Taggie stumbled past the fence Dad had half built. Ahead of her was the ring of ancient stone at the top of the well. Her leg felt awful, but she gritted her teeth and told herself the pain wasn't as bad as when she got clobbered by a hockey stick on the last game of term. They'd gone on to win that match.

'Taggie,' Jemima said in a shaky voice. 'Are you turning the lantern down?'

'No.' Even as she said it, she saw the lantern wasn't as bright as it had been when she switched it on.

'When did you wind it up last?'

'I can't remember.' The circle of light was visibly shrinking now.

'It doesn't matter,' Felix said. The squirrel leaned over the edge of the roundadown and dropped a tiny blue and white flower into the hole. '*Zarek fol*,' he murmured.

'Wind the lantern up again,' Jemima snapped.

'You have to switch it off to do that,' Taggie snapped back.

A loud rumbling sound came from the darkness of the roundadown. Taggie looked down to see a stone sliding out of the wall just below the rim. Then a second stone emerged slightly below the first and the next row down, and beyond that was a third, a fourth . . . It was like watching a spiral staircase growing down the well before her eyes.

'Leave the lantern on top,' Felix said in a rush. 'Come on, we haven't got much time left.' He sprang lightly on to the first stone, then began to scamper downwards, quickly passing into the darkness.

Taggie urged Jemima on to the top step. Jemima didn't need any further encouragement; shining her torch ahead, she hurried after Felix. Taggie placed the lantern on the rim, right by the top step, and started down, trying to avoid putting too much weight on her wounded leg. She had only gone round the wall a couple of times when the light above vanished. The low grinding sound came again, as the steps above began to retreat back into the curving walls. Taggie gulped and hurried on as fast as she could, trying to keep her footing true. She had no idea how far down the roundadown went.

Eventually she lost count of how many times she'd gone round. It was all she could do not to feel dizzy. And she was sure she could feel blood soaking into her sock below the dagger cut. Sometimes she caught a glimpse of Jemima's torch beam below, bobbing about as her sister scurried down and down.

Finally Jemima's beam was steady, and Taggie trotted down the last spiral, to land on a floor of dry leaves next to Felix. The sound of the steps retreating into the walls followed her, and less than half a minute later the bottom step had withdrawn, leaving a perfectly smooth curving wall of stone. She shone her torch round. There was a neat wooden doorway, bound with iron, inside an arching frame of stone. It was shut.

'There's no handle on the door,' Jemima said.

'The Great Gateways open only if they wish to,' Felix said. 'Ma'am, introduce yourself to Arasath.'

Taggie kept her torch beam on the wooden door. 'And it'll open?'

Felix's teeth chittered for a second. 'Yes. But you should know that sometimes the Great Gateways can be . . . troublesome.'

'What sort of troublesome?'

'Some are keen on making you solve riddles before they let you through. Others like a small gift. Some cause mischief for the sake of it. Some are jaded and require a tale of your travels to enliven their endless existence. Others lecture you for days, telling of how much better life was in times past. But not to worry – no Great Gateway would ever dare to turn you away.'

Taggie wasn't entirely convinced, but she stood in front of the door, squaring her shoulders. 'Hello. My name is Taggie, granddaughter of the Queen of Dreams, and I want to go to the First Realm where my father has been taken.'

Felix made a soft coughing sound, and his paw nudged Jemima.

'Oh. Hello, I'm Jemima, she's my grandma, too; and I want the same thing. I want my dad back.'

A cool dry gust of air stirred the leaves on the floor.

'The hope which your bloodline bestows to the First

Realm has been absent for a long time,' a deep voice said directly behind Taggie. She jumped and spun round, shining her torch against the blank wall to see who'd spoken. There was nobody there.

'It is Arasath who speaks,' Felix whispered.

Taggie gave him a confused glance. The white squirrel seemed to be a lot bigger in the dim light; his head came up to her elbow now.

'Will you bring it back, that hope?' the voice of Arasath asked gently. The Great Gateway sounded genuinely interested.

Taggie turned to the wooden door again. 'I want my father, that's all I know. What happens after I find him is something I do not know.'

'An honest answer,' Arasath said in amusement. 'That's something I haven't been given for a long time.'

'Please . . .' Taggie had to struggle to speak; there was a lump in her throat and she was worried she was about to start crying. It wasn't fair the Gateway was being so obstinate. *Why can't the wretched thing just open?* she thought. 'I just want to see him again. That's all.'

'All? You speak as if it were a trifle.'

'I'll do what I have to,' she said defiantly.

Felix's paw closed round her arm; she could feel his sharp claws through her sleeve. 'Be careful what you say,' he said quietly. 'And say little.'

'But you do not understand what it is that lies ahead of you,' Arasath murmured.

'I'll find out.'

'Honesty *and* determination. Your quest will be a grand one, I feel.'

'Thank you.' Taggie wasn't sure if that had been a compliment or not. She waited.

The leaves stirred briefly again. 'Would you like me to help?' Arasath asked smoothly.

'I . . . Yes, that would be kind. Thank you.'

'Polite as well. What a surprise. Welcome, lost princesses. Welcome to the First Realm, which is your birthright.'

The door began to swing back.

'Princess,' Jemima said wistfully. 'Did you hear that? Arasath called us princesses.'

Taggie gave her sister a gentle push through the now fully open door. There was a long brick tunnel behind it, curving sharply. Taggie limped on ahead, with Jemima next and Felix bringing up the rear. It was light in the tunnel, allowing Taggie to pocket her torch.

'That wasn't so difficult,' she said. 'How far to the other end?'

'That depends,' Felix said. 'Ma'am, it is unwise to confide so much to the Gateway. I did warn you they could be mischievous.'

'But we're through,' Jemima said breathlessly. 'We're in the First Realm. How amazing is that?'

Taggie thought they had walked almost a complete circle when a brighter light began to shine along the tunnel.

She hurried forward as best she could; her leg was aching badly now. There was one last turn and they came to the entrance. It was a similar door to the one at the bottom of the roundadown, and it was ajar. She pushed it open.

The sisters and Felix emerged into warm sunlight and the smell of a summer meadow. Beyond the doorway was a sight which Taggie simply wasn't prepared for. Ahead of her was a lush rolling landscape of fields and forests and rivers. The emerald panorama swept off into the far distance where details blurred into a single wash of green. Then, countless miles away, it began to curve upward like the wall of some giant valley. 'Oh gosh,' Taggie murmured in a very small voice. Her leg finally felt like it was about to give way, and she swayed alarmingly as she craned her head back. The ground of the First Realm stretched up and up, and still further up. Her mouth fell open as she followed the curve with her gaze, seeing a small sun directly overhead. Behind the sun, the First Realm kept on going, with mountains and plains and sparkling blue seas laid out as if it was a massive map forming the universe's biggest roof.

This realm was the exact opposite of the world she'd known all her life. Its lands were spread across the interior of a sphere, one that measured thousands of miles across.

Far above the ordinary clouds, long colourful streamers circled round the dazzling little sun that hung in the centre of the First Realm, casting massive black shadows over the lands that loomed directly above her head.

'I'm dreaming,' Jemima gasped, wiping a tear from her eye. 'It's amazing. Felix! Why didn't you tell us?'

Felix was staring up into the sky, with its weird shimmering multi-coloured clouds. His tail was rigid, with its fur all fluffed out. 'This is very wrong,' he said. 'This is not the First Realm I left two days ago. Then, the King of Night had smothered the sun and cursed the land with a fierce winter.' He turned round to face the door. 'Somehow, Arasath has deceived us.'

8

THE WRONG TIME

Taggie sat down hard. She simply couldn't stand up any more. Nervously she looked down at her leg. Her black jeans were glistening darkly with blood. She pressed her lips together and moaned, trying hard not to cry.

At once Felix was beside her. 'How bad is it?' he asked, full of concern.

'It hurts quite a bit,' she admitted reluctantly, hating how weak that made her sound. After all, the gnome's blade hadn't been that big.

'Those little brutes always drench their blades in wanspider venom to make the pain worse and stop the blood from clotting.' Felix looked worried.

'You mean they poisoned her?' Jemima squeaked.

'I fear so.' Felix carefully rolled up Taggie's jeans, exposing a long gash that was bleeding freely. 'I have some bandages and ointments . . . That will hold the damage for a while, but we need to get you to a mage or a healer.' He reached round and produced a small satchel. Like the sword, Taggie couldn't see where he'd kept it.

She screwed her eyes shut at the pain throbbing in her

leg. Jemima reached out a hand to touch the wound with a finger.

'Don't,' Taggie said instinctively. But Jemima's eyes were closed. Before Taggie could say anything further, she felt the hot pain diminish exactly where Jem was touching her, and sighed in relief. 'Oh, that's better,' she murmured.

'Hold still, ma'am,' Felix instructed. He'd produced a glass phial from his satchel and was about to pour the emerald-green potion over the gash.

Jemima blinked. 'No, wait,' she said in a dreamy voice. The palm of her hand pressed down on Taggie's leg.

'Jem?' Taggie asked uncertainly.

But Jem wasn't listening. Her eyes were tight shut. '*Ranoguil*,' she whispered.

Taggie and Felix peered down at the wound. A puff of noxious purple vapour was expelled, which Taggie guessed was the wanspider venom. Almost immediately she felt better, as if she'd managed to get her breath back. A cool sensation slithered up her leg.

'It's stopped – look,' Taggie said in astonishment.

Sure enough, the flow of blood slowed to a dribble and halted.

Jemima was holding her bloodied hand up in front of her face, as if she'd never seen it before. 'How did I do that? I didn't know I could do that.' She sounded almost scared.

Felix fixed his dark eyes on her. 'You have a healer's touch, Princess. It is only to be expected; many of your royal ancestors were renowned healers.'

Jemima's mouth curled up into a delighted grin. 'Oh, wow! That is so *cool*. I wonder if I can do any other spells?'

'Your abilities are waking, now you are in the First Realm. It is your heritage,' Felix said solemnly. 'And your destiny. Time will show us what both of you are capable of.'

The sisters looked at each other. Taggie grinned sheepishly. 'Thanks, Jem.'

She lay back on her elbows and let Felix wrap a slim bandage round the wound. High above, some white birds circled lazily. Above them were hazy clouds, and far, far above them, the strange stripes of dark-coloured cloud swirled slowly across the little sun. It was a warm day, with a scent of wildflowers in the air. She couldn't think of a more pleasing sight.

'Are all the Realms like this?' she asked.

'No,' Felix replied. 'They are all different. But this is the only one where you cannot see the stars.'

'Oh.' Taggie hadn't thought of that; it was almost disappointing. 'Why not?'

'It's said that when the angels brought people to the Realms at the start of the First Times, they folded the First Realm around itself so nothing else could follow them from the Heavens. That way the new people would always be safe.'

'Safe from what?' Jemima asked.

'Back then the gods themselves were at war among the stars,' Felix said. 'Angels and archangels fought terrible battles for them. But that ended long ago. Now we just fight among ourselves. And even the First Realm isn't safe.'

'How has Arasath deceived us?' Taggie asked, remembering Felix's words. Looking round at the incredible spherical landscape, she couldn't see anything amiss.

'I fear the Great Gateway has been dreadfully roguish,' Felix said. 'When you told Arasath you wanted to see your father, its reply – *Welcome to the First Realm, which is your birthright* – troubled me. Too glib. We will have to travel to the palace to confirm what I think has happened.'

'The palace,' Jemima said with a smile. 'Really?'

'Yes, Princess,' Felix said.

He held his paw out for Taggie. When she hauled herself back to her feet she realized that the squirrel was now only a few inches shorter than herself, and she was tall for her age. She chose not to mention it. After all of the shocking and bizarre things that had happened in the last couple of hours, a squirrel that magically changed size was the least of her worries.

'How far is the palace?' she asked.

Felix pointed to a line of hills that were heavily forested. 'Beyond those hills – perhaps a day's travel. And ma'am, would you please trust me when I say I think we should try to stay out of sight as much as possible?'

'Of course.'

Felix led them down a narrow path, in truth no more than a meandering track where the grass was slightly shorter than average. The meadowland on either side was speckled by wildflowers. They'd been walking for a minute when Jemima suddenly stopped and let out an excited cry. 'Taggie! Taggie, look.'

Taggie went over to her sister, who was kneeling, with her hands cupped together in front of her face. She was holding the long stalk of a giant poppy, with the scarlet petals inside her fingers. Taggie peered over her shoulder to see what all the fuss was about.

The petals were growing, starting to sway about gently even though there was no breeze. Taggie blinked in astonishment. What she'd thought of as petals were flapping now, and a moment later a gorgeous butterfly took flight, wobbling away through the air.

'Oh, Taggie . . .' There were tears in Jemima's eyes. 'Have you ever seen anything so pretty?'

'No,' Taggie admitted. Now she knew what to look for, she saw all the butterflies above the meadows were fluttering up from the flower stems that had birthed them. 'How does this happen?' she asked.

'They're just flutterseeds,' Felix said, sounding unimpressed. 'Don't you have them in the Outer Realm?'

'Not like this,' Taggie murmured.

They carried on down the path to a small, single-storey brick building. It looked very similar to a Victorian village railway station, even down to the platform with its wooden canopy. Instead of a metal track there was a canal. Felix checked the big clock on the wall, and consulted a timetable. 'The next turtle should be along soon,' he said.

By now, Taggie had learned not to question anything,

and sure enough, a few minutes later, an enormous turtle came paddling along the canal. It was as big as a double-decker bus, with a shell that was the colour of grubby brass. Cheerful blue-and-white-painted benches were fixed to the top, and a small wooden stair curved down the side.

It drew level with them. The huge fat neck curved round, and Taggie found herself looking into dark green eyes. 'All aboard,' the turtle hooted softly. It winked solemnly. Taggie grinned back, and scuttled up the narrow stairs.

Once they were all sitting on the front bench, the turtle started paddling again. It was surprisingly fast, and the meadows and fields were soon sliding past. Taggie was surprised by how much this part of the First Realm looked like the farmland around Grantham, with its neat little fields set out with dry stone walls, and lonely farmhouses glimpsed amid clumps of trees.

They passed through several deserted stations on the canal, then entered a big circular pond. It was a junction for six canals. Several other turtles were crossing, their benches full of passengers. Jemima did her best not to stare, but it was hard. A lot of the people were ordinary. *Or Outer Realm ordinary*, she told herself. She saw dwarfs and some tall skinny people like Mr Anatole, but with heads that were more animal than human. She gasped as she caught sight of some pig-nosed Rannalal, but these ones weren't wearing armour. Then there were blue, human-like creatures with four arms, and a couple of huge men with green hair. 'All giants have green hair,' Felix whispered, sensing Jemima's amazement. There were also one or two hulking shapes with scaly skin – 'trolls', Felix told her.

For all their differences, all the creatures chattered away merrily as their turtles carried them along. Jemima desperately wanted to wave and talk to them and tell them who she was, and how wonderful and exciting and colourful their Realm was, and how she wanted to live here rather than the world she grew up in, which now seemed so drab by comparison.

'They're all so happy,' Jemima said.

'Yes,' Felix said wistfully.

'But if this King of Night guy, Jothran, is ruining everything . . . how can it be so lovely here?' Jemima asked.

'He hasn't ruined anything yet,' Taggie said with a

sigh. She understood now what Arasath had done; Felix was right, it was *devious*. 'Arasath has sent us back in time. We're here *before* the Karrak Lords invade. This is the First Realm as it *should* be. Our birthright. Is that right, Felix?'

'I fear so, Princess, yes.'

'But how are we going to help Dad if we're lost in the past?' Jemima cried.

'I don't know,' the squirrel said, flicking his tail in agitation. 'But if anyone can give us advice we can trust, it is the Queen of Dreams.'

'Of course: Grandma,' Taggie said in delight.

'We're going to see Grandma?' Jemima asked.

'Indeed,' Felix replied.

As they crossed the pond, they drew a few interested gazes. Then their turtle swam into a canal on the other side, where the banks were closely planted with tall willows which shielded them from further view.

'The next station is Blogalham,' Felix said. 'It's quite a big town. I think we should get off before there and make the rest of our way on foot.'

The turtle slowed obligingly and they jumped from the bottom step to the grassy bank.

'Thank you,' Taggie said.

'You are welcome,' it replied.

Another turtle was two hundred yards behind them, and paddling along quickly.

'Come,' said Felix, and they hurried through the thick dangling boughs of the willows.

9

A JOURNEY THROUGH THE FIRST REALM

They walked for over an hour through gentle valleys and across fields and pastureland before finally reaching a forest of tall pines and lean silver birch trees. By now Taggie was desperately tired, and Jemima hadn't said a word for a long time, which was a sure sign of how exhausted she was. It was the bright sunlight that had fooled Taggie for a while, making her think it was still midday; but growing weariness soon reminded her that at Orchard Cottage it was now late at night.

'Felix, we need to rest,' Taggie finally said.

'Yes, of course. I'm sorry, I should have been more aware. There is a forest ranger's lodge not far away.'

Taggie looked up at the little sun burning bright directly overhead. 'Does night never come here?'

'Oh yes, the moonclouds swarm eternally, and bring night to every part of the First Realm. There –' he pointed upward – 'Fallanshire is in darkness, look. And over there, Gallbury sleeps. There, half the Estwial Sea is taken by night.'

Taggie followed his paw, and saw several vast patches of darkness across the land above. The country-sized shadows were cast from particularly dense clumps of the colourful cloud-web that caged the sun. 'Bring us the night,' she whispered to the moonclouds.

Felix had been right about their position. After just a few minutes' walk they came across a small glade. The lodge wasn't much – four low stone walls and a roof that looked like someone had simply dumped a pile of hay on the rafters – but Taggie had rarely been so relieved.

They were just going in when the light started to change. Jemima looked up to see a thick spiral of mooncloud sliding across the sun directly overhead. The front edge of the massive shadow that it cast was slithering fast across the land towards them, draining light from the sky above as it came. 'Oh good,' Jemima said. And a minute later both sisters were curled up on the floor, fast asleep.

Taggie woke to see bright slivers of sunlight slipping through the multitude of cracks in the door. Her stomach let out a loud rumble of complaint. She was terribly thirsty, too.

'I thought you might want a drink,' Felix said. He appeared, holding an ancient china jug and an equally old mug. 'There's a small spring on the other side of the clearing.' He poured some water out.

'Oh, thank you.' Taggie drank it down quickly.

Jemima woke, complaining about how hard the ground was to sleep on, then gulped down some water.

'I have found apples and some plums from the forest,'

Felix said. 'It is late in the season, but they are perfectly edible.'

Taggie never thought she'd be so grateful for apples at breakfast, but she munched them down, enjoying how good they tasted.

'It will take a couple of hours to reach the palace grounds from here,' Felix said as they emerged from the ranger's lodge. 'Fortunately, it sits on the edge of the city, so we can approach it through the parkland behind it.'

His head flicked round, scanning the surrounding trees.

'Come on!' Jemima said, and hurried off towards a gap in the trunks.

'Wait,' Taggie said in exasperation. 'You don't know where you're going.'

Felix used a slim claw to scratch his nose. 'Actually, that is the right way.'

'Oh,' Taggie mumbled. *How had Jem known that?* she wondered.

Jemima laughed, and stuck out her tongue.

Taggie tied her coat sleeves around her waist, and they set off along the narrow path Jemima had chosen. Within a couple of minutes they'd lost sight of the glade as the trees were so tall and closely packed. Wispy grass gave way to thick bracken, which clawed at their legs. Taggie was thankful she and Jemima were both wearing boots.

'What do you think our grandmother will say when she meets us?' Taggie asked as they walked.

'I have no idea, Princess,' Felix said.

'Do you think she'll believe us when we tell her we're her granddaughters?' Jemima said in a worried tone.

Felix looked back at Taggie. 'When we crossed the canal pond I assumed it was midday – there were no mooncloud shadows anywhere near us. Yet by the time we reached the lodge, the nightshadow had fallen. Did you do that, ma'am?'

'Er . . . I might have done,' Taggie said, looking worried.

'She's always cloudbusting at home,' Jemima said eagerly. 'Will she get into trouble for doing it here?'

'Jem! I'm not always doing it. And that wasn't busting – bringing the clouds together is the quite the opposite, actually.'

'Controlling the mooncl ouds is the duty of whoever sits upon the shell throne,' Felix said with a broad swish of his tail. 'Only your family has the gift. I expect your grandmother is quite curious to know who summoned the nightshadow early to this region. Not to mention everyone who was confused by an early evening, and is now having breakfast in what for them was supposed to be the middle of the night.'

'Oh . . .' A chastised Taggie concentrated hard on where she was putting her boots. How was she to know she could magic up night?

Finally the trees began to thin out again. They had gradually changed from the dark pines to grand oaks and copper beeches and elms. Now they opened out into a sweeping emerald parkland that extended for miles and miles. Taggie gasped at the city which marked the far side; its buildings were soaring towers and domes and elegant mansions more substantial and regal than anything she'd seen in cities back home. Sunlight sparkled off long crystal windows and gold-tipped spires.

'Lorothain,' Felix said with a happy sigh. 'Capital of the First Realm, and its most beautiful city. My family's home now.' He swiped a paw across his eyes. 'I didn't think I would see the First Realm like this again.'

Taggie put a reassuring hand on his shoulder, marvelling again at how soft his white fur was. 'Don't be sad, Felix. My grandmother will help us. I'm sure of it.'

'Of course, Princess. But this is hard ... seeing everything we've lost again. I would love to show you the splendour of Lorothain's boulevards and parks. You can't even see all of it from here. There is a big cliff in the Falsmu district where the river Trambor falls over a hundred and fifty metres to the lake below. And the airgardens on the cliff – aye, Princess Jemima would be in her element there.'

The sisters glanced at each other. For once Taggie didn't begrudge Jemima the insufferably proud smile.

They set out across the rich parkland. A mass of wildflowers had opened to greet the sun, creating a shimmering ripple of colour. More than once Taggie turned a full circle just to marvel at the sight of the flutterseeds beating their erratic way upward. There were far more behind than ahead.

Then she saw something else swish through the air,

swooping behind a huge beech tree – something a lot bigger than any butterfly or flutterseed, and *very* pink.

'Felix, there's something flying about over there.' As she said it, she saw two more creatures glide quickly out of sight. They seemed to leave a narrow wake of shimmering air behind them.

'Yes?' Felix said in a voice that was seriously unimpressed. 'The young skymaids often fly in the park. Pay them no heed.'

'Skymaids?' Jemima's jaw dropped open. 'Do you mean *fairies*?'

Felix merely grunted.

Taggie heard giggling coming from behind a broad oak tree. 'Hello?' she ventured.

Three young skymaids drifted out from behind the tree. They were nearly as tall as Jemima, but thinner, with limbs that were almost translucent, weirdly reminding her of jellyfish. They had big, triangular, fin-like feet that were mostly feathers; and their fingers were long and flat, with feathery edges. Fluffy hair floated slowly around their heads. It was all very interesting, Taggie thought, except for their clothes, which were

gauzy pink dresses, or topaz, or aquamarine. Delicate chains of glossy leaves were woven into their waving hair, or worn as bracelets and necklaces. She'd stopped wearing anything that girlishly frilly after her seventh birthday. But these skymaids looked very young, no more than five or six years old.

'Welcome, welcome,' they chanted, amid more giggling, as they drifted forward. 'Girls in such strange clothes.'

They were elegant in flight, Taggie had to admit, with wings sprouting from their shoulder blades, but always moving so fast they looked like nothing more than hazy patches of air. As they flew, little flicks of their feet helped guide them in gentle curves and even loops. They left a faint shimmer in the air behind them as they went, like a twinkling contrail.

'You're wonderful!' Jemima exclaimed. 'You're so magical.'

'They can fly because they're so light,' Felix said gruffly. 'They're certainly not weighed down by a brain.'

The skymaids circled round an enraptured Jemima, twirling as they went. 'Welcome, welcome,' they chorused. 'Such strange girls.'

'We're not strange,' Jemima said. 'We're visitors, that's all. I've never been to the First Realm before.'

'How lucky you are,' the pinkest one sang. 'This is the finest of all the Realms.'

'What do you do? Do you fly about all day? Where do you go?' asked Jem, breathlessly.

'We play with the birds.'

'And tease the cygnets.'

'And sip nectar from the treetops.'

'That's so lovely,' Jemima said with a sigh. 'Can I join you? Can you carry me?'

There was a fresh burst of giggling, and the skymaids circled higher and faster, then looped round to cluster about Jemima again. 'Heavy, heavy visitor, alas, we cannot lift such a weight.'

Jemima pouted.

'Princess Jemima,' Felix said. 'We really don't have time.'

'Yes, come on, Jem,' Taggie said reluctantly.

They set off again, with the skymaids flashing around them, sometimes swooping up high above the trees before laughing and plunging down again. The incessant giggling was starting to get annoying.

'Go away,' Felix told them crossly.

The skymaids laughed gently, and dropped green acorns on his fur, darting away quickly when he tried to swat at them. Eventually they flew off back to the trees that bordered the parkland, much to Felix's relief. 'Not much further now,' he said.

10

GRANDMA

Taggie spotted the palace when they were still a mile away. It was just as it appeared in her dreams: a sprawling building of white stone, with many courtyards and big halls, and turrets spaced regularly along the outer walls, all of which covered an area the same sort of size as Melham village. And a lot more besides if you counted the formal gardens that surrounded it.

'I wasn't expecting it to be so big,' Taggie said in awe.

One of the towers in the middle was twice as high as all the others.

'That's Queen Layawhan's Tower,' Felix said. 'It was built a thousand years ago in honour of those who fell at the Battle of Rothgarnal. It is the tallest tower in the First Realm.'

The three of them scrambled up the dry grassy ditch that marked the boundary of the gardens, and on to a lawn surrounded by a six-metre-high yew hedge. Several fountains sprayed water in stone-lined ponds. The sound of children playing came over the hedge. An open archway cut into the yews led through to another, much smaller garden boxed in by a beech hedge. Big chestnut and walnut trees cast a gentle dappled shade over the untidy grass. When Taggie peered cautiously round the corner of the archway, the thing that drew her eye was a tree house in one of the walnut trees; from what she could see of it, beneath its shaggy coat of purple-flowering vine, it was as old as the tree itself. She immediately wanted to scoot up the steep steps, and take in the view from the veranda. What grand times she and Jem could have playing in that, she thought.

'Taggie!' Jemima hissed at her side. 'There's Dad!'

Five small boys were playing football in the garden, running round enthusiastically after an inflated purple-and-white toadstool that wasn't quite spherical – which led to some interesting bounces.

'How would you know what Dad looked like when he was younger?' Taggie asked crossly. Even as she said it, she realized how strange it was that she'd never seen any photos of Dad when he was a boy.

'It's him,' Jem insisted, folding her arms across her chest, and getting ready to argue. 'I just *know*.'

Taggie took another look at the boy Jem had pointed at. He was about ten years old, and dressed in a fine gold-and-blue waistcoat, white satin shirt, and grey trousers streaked with mud. She had to admit, his features were kind of familiar.

'Daddy?' Taggie whispered. It was so hard to picture this carefree, laughing boy as her father. She'd never thought of him as anything other than a grown-up, all serious with responsibility. But here and now she felt as though she could go over and talk to him as an equal. But some strange feeling was holding her back. And not just her, by the look of things. Impulsive 'I-don't-care' Jem was also hovering this side of the archway, a look of desperation on her face.

'No,' Felix said sternly, his paws closing round both their wrists. 'This boy prince is not yet your father. You may not meet him. Not here. Not now.'

Taggie slowly nodded her head. 'OK.'

'Felix, please,' Jemima said in her worst whiney voice. 'Please, *please?*'

'I'm sorry, but we must go to the Queen now,' the squirrel said, and his tail drooped in sympathy. 'You cannot meet the boy prince, one wrong word could change time, throwing every Realm into chaos and ruin.'

Taggie took one last look at the laughing boy who would one day become her father as he tackled one of his friends. 'Love you, Daddy,' she whispered, and she turned to leave.

'Are *you* doing that, Princess Taggie?' Felix asked. He was tilting his head back, looking up at the sky suspiciously.

'Doing what?' Taggie asked.

'Bringing the moonclouds back.'

'No.'

The three of them stood still, puzzled as the light started to fade around them. Yet, above the hedge, the rooftops and turrets and domes of the palace continued to bask in bright sunlight.

Jemima rubbed her arms, suddenly chilly. 'What's happening?'

Felix raised his head, his small dark nose sniffing the air. 'There is magic swelling here.'

Taggie's gaze was drawn to the grand old trees in the garden, where the boys were playing. The canopy of verdant leaves and brawny boughs blocked the sunlight underneath, creating a veil of darkness that seemed to occupy the very air itself. As she watched, the edge of the shadows began to creep outward, rippling across the grass like a black puddle, spreading out to join those emerging from around the other trees. More shadows were also oozing out from the base of the hedge.

'What's doing this?' she asked.

'A mage must be shadecasting,' Felix said. 'And a powerful mage at that.' He drew his sword; the blade was shimmering with a pale green light.

The five boys playing football had fallen silent. They stood still, uncertain what to do as they watched the shadows grow closer and closer. In another minute the entire garden would be in shade. They began to huddle together in the last splash of sunlight.

'What shall we do?' Jemima asked.

'We have to warn Dad,' Taggie said abruptly.

'You *can't*!' Felix insisted.

'But—' Taggie broke off as she saw an unpleasantly familiar shape slip between the tree trunks. Four little legs scuttling along, red armour almost black in the dwindling light. Visor open to show a fat pig-like snout.

'Rannalal!' Taggie yelled out in warning.

Felix spun round, his sword ready, tail quivering tall. '*Quovak Acran!*' he said in a loud clear voice. Somewhere in the distance a bell started to ring. 'The palace alarm,' he explained. 'Help will be here in a moment. Princesses, you stay here, I'll protect the boy prince until the palace guard arrive. I belong here, even though not now.'

Taggie clenched her fists in frustration, but nodded agreement.

Felix went through the archway, and hurried towards the boys, his tail still and horizontal as he ran. 'Prince Dino,' he called out. 'I am an agent of the palace guard, you and your friends are in danger. Follow me, quickly, please.'

Taggie watched her young dad give a startled gasp as Felix bounded over the grass. Then something silver came spinning out of the tree shadows.

'Look out!' she cried.

A spinning net tangled round Felix, who fell with an angry cry. Heedless of the danger, Taggie sped over to the stricken squirrel.

Felix was struggling furiously under the slim strands of the net, which was now contracting. 'I can't move to cut it,' he growled. The net had pinned his sword by his side. Taggie gripped one of the strands and tried to break it, the strand was so thin it should have been easy, but it was too strong. She pushed her hand through the net, and tried to pull Felix's sword free.

'Look out!' Jemima called. 'I can see more.'

Taggie snatched a quick glance, but there were no Rannalal in sight. She just managed to get her fingers round the sword hilt, and pulled. It came free, slicing through several strands as it moved. Felix shoved a paw through the gap.

'A Rannalal,' Prince Dino gasped.

Taggie twisted round in time to see another Rannalal knight burst through the shadows engulfing the hedge, running swiftly towards the group of boys on its four stout legs. One hand held a wicked axe, the other swung a silver net above its head.

'No!' Taggie yelled. She raced across the lawn towards the Rannalal knight. Her thoughts were perfectly calm as she remembered Mr Koimosi's martial arts instructions. *Balance on the left foot, bend, coil, focus, and kick.* Her right boot caught the Rannalal knight on the side of his stumpy neck, sending him flying. The net flapped about chaotically and Taggie dodged it gracefully, allowing it to wrap itself around the groaning Rannalal as he tumbled to the ground, his armour clanging louder than the bell.

Jemima kicked the sword out of his hand.

'Wow!' Prince Dino said. He was staring at the downed Rannalal in amazement. 'How did you do that? It was totally fantastic.'

Now his paws and sword were free, Felix cut off the rest of the net. Two more Rannalal emerged from the hedge's

77

cloying shadows. Felix leaped towards them. His glowing sword sliced straight through a heavy wooden baton with a loud rasping sound. Then his free paw made a throwing motion, and a tiny, shining red disc went shimmering through the air like a sizzling star. It struck a Rannalal knight on his chest, smashing him high into the air. He wailed frantically, all four legs waggling wildly as he tumbled over the hedge.

The shadows were growing stronger, sucking light from the air as they constricted round Taggie and the boys. She felt something like frost settling on her skin, stealing the warmth from her flesh. More insubstantial shapes were flitting through the shadows behind the trees. Tiny violet sparks skittered about. She knew they were the glowing eyes of the Rannalal, and soon more nets would come whirling out of the darkness. Too many for her and Felix to fight off alone.

Instinctively Taggie knew this ambush wasn't something you could run from or fight with swords and kicks. She was in the First Realm now. Her true home. This was magic she was up against. It had to be matched and beaten.

Then she glimpsed a single ghostly shape growing out of the darkness that was wrapping itself inexorably around her. Except that it wasn't a shape, she realized, but a memory that wasn't hers. An eye sketched by slender blue lines; and she'd seen that eye before.

She held up her arm with Dad's charm bracelet. Sure

enough, the exact same symbol was on one of the bands, glowing a sharp blue.

When she looked at other symbols on the bracelet, she saw that several had also begun to glow with colours of their own. Instinctively she reached out with her other hand, and started to turn the bands. It was like a circular version of a Rubik's cube. Somewhere in her head was a memory of how the symbols ought to be aligned to banish the shadows.

She thrust out her right hand, pointing without hesitation where she now knew the shadecaster to be, skulking behind a walnut tree next to the hedge. '*Derat al-tooman*,' she called, the enchantment for clear sight. A thin light shone through the symbols as she felt strange forces flow inside her.

The shadows summoned by the shadecaster popped like a soap bubble as the sunlight which had been subtly lured away from the garden snapped back. A furious groan rumbled through the air. Five Rannalal stumbled to a halt as the newly blazing sunlight exposed them, blinking eyes peering out through their narrow visor slits; uncertain what to do now their advantage was lost. Then two of them ran forward, screaming ferociously as they came.

Taggie flinched. The Rannalal knights might be small, but they were armed, and trained. And heading straight at her.

She knew at once which of the charm bracelet's symbols should be aligned: rock paired with wind. And there they were, glowing on bands that spun to place them together. In her mind she heard someone chanting, a deep commanding voice. '*Israth hyburon,*' she repeated. Her whole arm shone a vivid orange. She punched forward.

The air in front of her rippled.

An invisible force hit the Rannalal knights, sending both of them flying backwards, spinning end over end before they thudded down hard into the ground. One groaned in pain and tried to lift himself before collapsing back down. The other never moved.

'Huh!' Taggie exclaimed. She stared at her arm, which was now perfectly ordinary again. No orange glow anywhere.

The remaining Rannalal knights looked at Felix, who was approaching them, glowing sword held ready. Then they looked at Taggie, seeing the content expression spreading across her face as she began to close her hand into a fist again, and started to back away.

'Enough.' A soft voice tinkled round the garden.

Taggie felt an overwhelming sense of peace embrace her and sighed in relief. It was all she could do not to give a huge yawn, so relaxing was the sweet enchantment. Indeed, she watched the Rannalal knights fall slowly to the ground as sleep claimed them. The texture of the sunlight changed, growing warm and rosy.

The Queen of Dreams walked through the gate in the hedge, dressed in a flowing blue and white dress, a simple tiara of flowers in her hair. Taggie caught sight of Jemima staring at her worshipfully, as if she couldn't quite believe what she was seeing.

'Mother,' the young prince shouted, and ran to the Queen of Dreams. Her arms folded him safely to her.

'There, there, Dino, it is over now,' the Queen soothed her son.

Palace guards hurried into the garden behind their Queen. Taggie was taken aback by the sight of them. They were big men with four arms each, emerging from broad double shoulders, which allowed them to carry two shields and two weapons at the same time. Their white and silver armour shone in the sun, making them look imposing and noble at the same time; and each helmet had an ice-blue open-shell crest at the front.

Taggie watched impassively as four armed guards (Holvans, Felix told her) surrounded each of the sleeping Rannalal knights and disarmed them. Five more of them closed in on the dazed mage who had woven the shadecast. Taggie was curious to see him. He was a young man, wearing short brown robes and gold chains. His face, with its wild eyes and eyebrows scrunched together, had a permanently furtive expression. As the palace guards led him away he gave Taggie a sullen, fearful look.

The Queen came over to where Felix, Taggie and Jemima were standing in a nervous little huddle. 'Now who do we have here?' she enquired keenly.

'Majesty,' Felix stammered, bowing low. 'I am Felix, a special agent of the royal palace guard.'

'And one of the Weldowen family, I believe,' the Queen of Dreams said with a smile. 'But, strangely, I do not know you.'

'Not yet, Majesty,' Felix said. 'Sadly there is dark wizardry afoot today. I came here to seek your urgent advice on the matter. But I would politely request that Prince Dino is taken to the safety of the palace. There are things today that he should not see or hear.'

'Of course.'

'But Mother!' Dino protested.

'I know,' the Queen of Dreams said, clapping her hands. 'But it is for the best, I feel.' Several courtiers appeared in the gateway behind her. 'Go now. All you boys. Such an adventure you have had.'

Taggie watched her young dad stiffen stubbornly. *Gosh, just like Jemima*, she thought. Then he turned to face her, which she wasn't expecting, and his face had an awed look. 'You saved me,' he said to her. 'Thank you. I owe you my life.'

'Come along.' The Queen beckoned a courtier.

'I've never seen anyone do that,' the young prince exclaimed. 'It was incredible. You kicked the Rannalal as if you were in a dance. And your magic is so strong.'

Felix came to stand in front of Taggie, blocking her from view. 'Say nothing,' he cautioned quietly.

'Who are you?' the young prince asked desperately. The courtiers started to bustle him away. 'Please?'

Taggie tried to peer round Felix's tail.

'Please, lady, you saved me. At least tell me your name.'

'You'll know one day,' Taggie burst out. Felix looked at her sharply.

'But—' And the boy prince was gone, pushed through the gate and away towards the palace.

The Queen of Dreams embraced the sisters. 'I understand who you are, which makes this so hard for both you and me,' she said gently. 'And I can bring no comfort to either of you, for you are but visitors to this place and time. But know this: I am proud to have met you this day, beloved granddaughters.'

11

WHAT DO WE DO NOW?

The Queen of Dreams led the sisters and Felix up the steep rickety wooden steps into the tree house. 'I loved playing here when I was your age,' she told them. 'My friends would be with me, and the skymaids would visit often, and the centaurs, and – oh, so many people.' She sighed. 'So many delightful games. So much fun. Happy times. And we had food, too, such feasts. Dino doesn't use it much – he's always so busy playing football with his friends.' She signalled one of the courtiers down in the garden. 'Bring something to eat – these dear girls look famished.'

Inside the tree house was a wooden table very similar to the one in Orchard Cottage's kitchen. Windows in the roof were partially covered with the sweet-smelling vine flowers, allowing broad splinters of light to shine down through the gaps. A big cupboard stood against the back wall.

'Majesty,' Felix began when they were sitting at the table. 'I apologize again for bringing the princesses here to you but—'

'A Great Gateway thought otherwise,' the Queen said with a knowing smile.

'Yes, Majesty,' Felix admitted.

'Which one?'

'Arasath.'

'Of *course*. Arasath always claims it does what is best for the First Realm.'

Felix twitched his nose uncertainly. 'I don't see how it could be for the best, my Queen. We are from the future. We should not be here. I came to ask you what we should do.'

'What did Arasath say?'

'I believe it wanted Princess Taggie to see her true birthright, the First Realm, before it . . .' He fell silent as the Queen raised her hand.

'You know you cannot speak to me of what is to come. Fate and destiny cannot be altered; what will be, is; all the Realms will suffer if these most basic laws are broken. And I – I do not wish to know what fate has in store for me. That would be the cruellest knowledge.'

'I understand, my Queen.'

'But it is most strange that Arasath would allow those Rannalal and their mage to follow you. There is a Dark Lord behind this, you say?'

'Yes, my Queen.'

'Who knows what wizardries they possess. In the meantime we will care for the Rannalal with utmost compassion, and trust that in time they may come to abandon their wicked ways.' The Queen gave the sisters a mournful look. 'You poor things. You look like you've been through such an ordeal.'

'We have,' Jemima said. 'It was awful, I never knew Dad was a prince, or that we would—'

'No,' the Queen said firmly. 'I'm sorry, but I cannot know of your quest. Already, what I've seen is greatly perturbing to me. Princesses of the First Realm pursued by Darkness through a Great Gateway from the Outer Realm. Difficult times clearly lie ahead.'

'But Grandma, I don't know what we have to do,' Taggie said. 'We thought you could help us.' She'd been expecting the Queen to tell them how to find their father, how to defeat the Karrak Lords and restore the First Realm to what it should be. A few of those tough-looking four-armed Holvan palace guards to escort them on the journey might be nice too. Instead she got nothing but good wishes! It wasn't fair – not after everything they'd seen and done already.

The Queen of Dreams took her hand and those irresistible blue eyes looked into hers. 'All I can do is show you the road home. I think you know what you have to do when you get there, Taggie, dear. What you fear is how your task must be accomplished now you have seen the true nature of the Realms. That I fully understand and sympathize with. But I could never help you with that, now could I?'

Taggie dropped her head. 'No,' she mumbled. 'But I don't know how to do what I have to. I don't know anything. Please, Grandma, you have to help us.'

'You are a Princess of the First Realm; do not underestimate yourself,' the Queen said. 'I just saw you counter-charm the shadecast of a fully trained adult mage. That is no mean feat for someone your age.'

'I don't know how I did that,' Taggie protested. She stared crossly at the charm bracelet. 'This bracelet guided me.'

'Not entirely,' the Queen said. 'The bracelet, or rather the *charmsward* you wear, was shaped by Usrith, our family's father, a mage of the First Times. It was he who forged the shell throne which tamed this Realm and made it the sweetest of all the lands to live in.'

Taggie looked at the charm bracelet again. 'But I still don't get how I used it. Can you teach me to do it properly?'

'I don't have to. That is the beauty of the charmsward – it only ever binds with someone from our bloodline, someone with a good heart, and someone with magical ability. It chose you, Taggie, for you are all of those things. And you must never worry about how to use it, for it carries with it memories from past wearers. These will mingle with your own thoughts, so you have only to ponder the type of enchantment you need and you'll remember how to cast it.'

'Oh that's so cool,' Taggie gave the bracelet a more appreciative look.

A courtier came in carrying trays of food and a large bowl of nuts for Felix. Jemima let out an appreciative sigh and started munching through the sandwiches, only taking time off to gulp down the cool elderflower drink.

The Queen gave Taggie a secretive little smile and raised her right arm so the sleeve of her robe fell back, revealing the charmsward around her own wrist. 'I sometimes wear it myself,' the Queen said.

Taggie drew a sharp breath. Of all the strangeness from travelling back in time, seeing the charmsward on her wrist and her grandmother's *at the same time* was definitely the weirdest.

'Though I dislike some of the spells it knows,' the Queen continued. 'So you see, part of my essence will be with you on your quest.'

'Thank you.' Taggie smiled round a slice of the juiciest honey melon she'd ever tasted.

'All Dad left *me* was some money,' Jemima said in a disappointed tone as she held up the suede purse.

The Queen smiled. 'Oh Jemima, what a bright hot fire you are. How you will delight those who know you.'

Jemima blushed, unable to meet her grandmother's intense gaze.

'But you judge your father falsely,' the Queen chided. 'He loves you too much to simply buy your happiness. Have you forgotten what else is in the purse? I can sense the seers' runes from here. Unless I'm very much mistaken, they are the ones that belonged to my cousin Ballania. Oh, the mischief she and I got up to together when we were your age!'

Jemima scrambled through the coins in the purse, anxiously retrieving the old stone dice. 'Do you mean these?' she asked excitedly.

'Yes.'

'I didn't know they were runes.' Jemima pursed her lips together in puzzlement. 'What do I do with them?'

'You throw them to see,' the Queen told her.

'See what?'

'What you want to see. What you need to see. If you have the sight.'

Jemima quickly flung them on to the table, and studied the tiny symbols intently. They were mostly parallel lines, little more than crude scratches. 'What do they show?'

'They only ever reveal their meaning to the seer to whom they belong.'

'But I can't *see* anything!'

The Queen ruffled her hair. 'Patience. Though even without runes I can see how hard that will be to your nature. You must practise long and hard. Seers always say they never perfect their art in their lifetime, they only ever improve.'

Jemima became sulky again, putting the runes back into her suede purse.

'And you, Felix Weldowen,' the Queen said. 'What have you to ask me?'

Felix's tail fluffed out as he bowed. 'Nothing, Majesty. It is my honour to serve the Queen of Dreams.'

'Your loyalty deserves some reward. I see you have endured much in pursuit of your duty.' The Queen slipped a plain gold ring from her finger. 'If you need comfort in dark times, if you need soothing when there seems to be no hope, I will be with you and do my best to ease your suffering.'

Felix bowed again, the tip of his tail quivering as he slipped the ring on his paw. 'Majesty.'

'And now you must be on your way,' the Queen said. 'In that at least I can help you.' She got up and tapped lightly on the cupboard doors at the back of the tree house. 'Taslaf, you will return these fine girls to the Realm where they were born.'

'As you wish, Majesty,' a voice said behind Taggie. She jumped, but of course there was no one there.

The cupboard doors opened silently, revealing a

wooden spiral staircase behind.

'Taslaf is another of the Great Gateways,' the Queen said. 'It will take you back to the Outer Realm. And it *certainly* won't let anyone follow you back.'

'Quite so,' Taslaf said in a haughty voice.

'However,' the Queen continued, 'be careful when you get there. You will have to go back to Orchard Cottage and confront Arasath, for *only* Arasath can undo the mischief it has created.' She held Taggie's hands. 'Be firm with it, be resolute about who you *really* are, and make sure it fully knows that too.'

'Yes, Grandma.'

The Queen kissed her, then turned to Jemima. 'So little time is a dreadful crime, but I am grateful to have had these few minutes with you. Be strong, my bright little fire, know that I love you now and always.'

Jemima hugged the Queen of Dreams tightly. 'I don't want to go.'

'I know,' the Queen replied sadly.

Their hug went on for a long time. Taggie eventually took Jemima's hand and led her through the door.

'And remember to practise your sight,' the Queen called out as they started to climb the stairs.

'I will,' Jemima promised.

The spiral stairs stretched up a lot higher than those in the roundadown of Orchard Cottage, and certainly taller than the tree they'd started inside. After a couple of minutes the light began to fade around them, not that Taggie had ever seen where it was coming from. She took her torch out and began climbing again. Several spirals later she realized the steps were now cast iron rather than wood, and the walls were brick.

Abruptly she came to a door with a large brass handle. She could just make out muffled sounds on the other side.

'Felix?' she said softly. 'What do I do?' She looked round and saw that he'd shrunk in size again; he was almost as small as a real Outer Realm squirrel now.

'Open it,' he said simply.

Carefully she turned the handle. The door opened inwards a couple of inches. A dreary grey daylight spilt through the crack. There was no one directly outside, so she pulled the door back.

The sound of traffic was the first thing she noticed, though there was something oddly grating about the engine noise, as if sand had got into the gears. Directly opposite her was a brick wall, darkened by grime. It had an alcove in it, the same shape as the doorway she stood in. The ground in front was some kind of sloping cobbled road with two sets of iron rails running along it. To her right was the rectangular entrance to a tunnel. They'd come out halfway along a ramp that led up to ground level. When she looked up she could see buildings and trees above the railings that lined the top of the ramp wall.

'Quickly,' Taggie urged.

'What is this place?' Jemima asked, peering up at the railings.

'A city somewhere,' Taggie said. 'Come on.' She started up the ramp, towards the sound of traffic and people. Felix scooted directly up the vertical brick wall without any difficulty. Then he was running along the top of the railings, head swivelling from side to side.

'What's up there?' Taggie asked him.

Before he could answer, a bell sounded. It was brash and insistent. Taggie glanced over her shoulder and yelped. An old-fashioned tram was trundling out of the tunnel behind them, the driver glaring at them as his arm pulled the bell chord.

'Run!' Taggie shouted. She and Jemima pelted up the ramp with the tram closing on them, bell still clanging wildly. They reached the end of the railings, and dived sideways. A car horn hooted. Taggie grabbed Jemima's hand and tugged her forward on to the closest pavement. Only then did they stop, hearts pounding, and take a good look around.

They'd come out at a broad road intersection, with the tramlines curving round to the right, and cars and buses trundling about, seemingly in every direction. The cars were all ancient, small and drab-coloured, with narrow spoke wheels. Buses were similarly old-fashioned.

'What's happened to all the windows?' Jemima said in puzzlement. 'They've all got crosses on them.'

Taggie saw what she meant. Every window along the

city street had white tape stuck across it. Then she noticed the people walking past were giving the sisters curious, semi-suspicious stares. The clothes the women wore were the kind her mum's *Vogue* magazine had shown in their 1940s retro feature the other week. And most of the men seemed to be in military uniforms. She suddenly realized what the Queen of Dreams had meant when she said: '*Only Arasath can undo the mischief it has created.*'

'Oh no!' she groaned. 'We're still in the past. We need to get back to Orchard Farm and go through Arasath to get back to our own time.'

She looked round, trying to work out where they were. The street sign on the corner of the intersection read 'Southampton Row WC1'. She knew that was a London sign.

Jemima was tugging her arm.

'What?' Taggie snapped.

A very subdued Jemima simply pointed up into the sky. Taggie followed the line of her finger. A huge grey oval balloon with three fat fins at the rear was floating above the rooftops. More were visible across the skyline behind it.

'Where are we?' Jemima asked in a small voice.

'London,' Taggie told her. 'During the Blitz.'

12

A CITY AT WAR

'I'll keep look-out,' Felix said to the sisters as they stared round in surprise at the wartime city. He jumped on to the wall of the shop behind them, and scaled it effortlessly, jumping across window ledges, then scampering up a drainpipe with his tail waggling energetically as he went. When he reached guttering he leaned over and raised a paw. Taggie was sure it was a thumbs-up gesture, and hoped no one else had seen. The last thing they needed now was people asking them difficult questions – any questions at all, actually.

She and Jemima walked for fifteen minutes, taking a route along Bloomsbury Way and out on to Oxford Street. Taggie had been to London dozens of times; she even remembered visiting department stores along Oxford Street. But there was no Centre Point tower, no small noisy tourist shops with 'I LOVE LONDON' T-shirts, mugs and tea towels. It was so different to the London she knew, so drab and depressing. People gave her and Jemima curious glances, almost frowning at their bright coats.

'What are we going to do?' Jemima asked.

'We have to get back to Orchard Cottage and Arasath,' Taggie said.

'But how? Melham is over a hundred miles away.'

Taggie stopped in the middle of the pavement. As she tried to work out just how they could travel back to Melham an acorn landed on her head.

'Ow!' Taggie looked up to see Felix peering over the guttering, wearing his purple glasses. His paw was jabbing out urgently. She followed the gesture.

On the other side of the road there was a man in a long black leather coat and a trilby hat. He was looking directly at her and Jem. His hat cast a shadow over his face, so all she could see of his features was a pair of wire-rimmed glasses. Something about him unnerved her.

'Come on, let's keep moving,' she said.

'But how do we get there?' Jemima insisted.

'Think about it: the railway lines are still the same,' Taggie replied, rather pleased with herself. 'We'll go to King's Cross station and catch a train up to Grantham. After that, we'll walk the rest of the way if we have to. It's only ten miles.'

'All right. But how do we buy a ticket?'

It was all Taggie could do not to stomp her foot. Did the pestering questions never end?

'You've got money. Remember? The kind of money that people always accept: gold.'

'Do they take that at railway ticket offices? In wartime?'

'Jem, will you stop trying to rubbish everything I say.'

96

'I'm not. I'm just saying you need real Outer Realm money to buy anything *in* the Outer Realm.'

'Really? And since when have you started calling this the Outer Realm?'

'Since I found out that's what it is. And you haven't answered my question.'

'It's very simple, actually.'

'Oh yeah?'

'Yeah.' Taggie squared her shoulders, trying desperately to think.

'How then?' Jemima asked sneeringly.

An old memory came slithering to the rescue. 'Jewellers buy gold,' Taggie said, trying not to sound relieved. 'We just have to find one.'

'There's one over there,' Jemima pointed behind her.

'Huh?'

Even Jemima looked surprised at what she'd done. She peered down the street. 'There.'

The jewellery shop was a hundred metres away. Taggie's eyes narrowed with suspicion. But there was no way she was asking Jemima how she had known it was there. That would have been admitting defeat. 'Well spotted, Jem,' was all she'd allow herself to say.

They hurried forward. Taggie made a series of what she hoped were unobtrusive hand signals to Felix, who was loping along the rooftops above them. Then she wondered if Felix actually got that five fingers splayed out meant five minutes. Oh well, he was magical – he'd work it out.

The jeweller's shop was as dreary on the inside as it was on the out. Wood-framed display cases showed off a small collection of rings and necklaces. The one for watches was half empty. A single yellow light bulb hanging from the ceiling was the only illumination.

The man behind the counter frowned when they came in, giving Taggie's quilted orange coat a long look. Eventually he said: 'Yes, young ladies, what can I do for you?'

'I was wondering if you bought gold coins?' Taggie asked in her sweetest voice. She held out the smallest of Jemima's collection.

The jeweller's eyebrows shot up in in amazement. 'Where did you get this?'

'It was my grandmother's,' said Jemima, who was now also being as charming as possible. 'She left it to me.'

'I see,' the shopkeeper said. 'Does she travel abroad a lot?'

'She may do,' Taggie said, reluctant to give details. 'Please, will you buy it?'

'I wish I could,' he said, scratching the back of his head. 'But it's not something I deal in.'

'Oh. Do you know anyone who does?' asked Jem.

'That'll be Mr Glenton. He has a shop in Covent Garden. He's interested in foreign coins.'

'Thank you so much,' Taggie said with a smile.

The jeweller consulted his watch. 'He'll be closing up now. But he opens at half nine sharp in the morning.'

'We have to wait until the morning? Why, what time is it?'

'Half past five.' The jeweller was staring at her watch, which was just visible below her coat cuff. Taggie realized it was the one with a liquid crystal display – and they certainly never had those during the Second World War.

'Of course,' she said. 'Thank you for your help. We'll be going now.'

They started walking to the door.

'Where did you say you were from?' the jeweller asked.

'Grantham,' Jemima said at exactly the same time that Taggie said: 'King's Cross.'

'Um, that is, we were evacuated from King's Cross to Grantham,' Taggie said hurriedly. 'Goodbye.'

'What did you say King's Cross for?' Jemima hissed when they were outside.

'I . . .' Taggie looked back through the glass door, to see the jeweller lifting up a telephone. 'It didn't make sense to say somewhere outside London.'

'We could be visiting. We *are* visiting.'

'Come on.' Taggie pulled at Jemima's arm, wanting to get a long way from the jeweller's.

'Now what?' Jemima grumbled.

'The shopkeeper is suspicious. It's wartime: people are suspicious about anything out of the ordinary.' As she said it she looked back and saw the man in the leather coat again. Her breath caught in her throat. He was there, along with someone who could have been his twin. They were both wearing identical black leather coats and trilbies, the setting sun reflecting off their glasses. She began to think no one else could see them. Other pedestrians were walking past the leather coats without even glancing at them.

'Let's go,' Taggie insisted. She glanced up, relieved to see a flash of white fur on the roof above.

The sisters set off down Oxford Street. It was getting noticeably darker now as the sun sank below the rooftops. Smoke was pouring out of every chimney, bringing the strong bitter smell of coal to the air. Buses and army trucks rumbled along the road, puffing out fumes. London had never smelt so bad when she visited. And now she was really looking round, Taggie noticed every building was coated in soot and grime.

'What are we going to do until morning?' Jemima asked.

'I don't know. I suppose we can sleep on a park bench.'

'Really? Did they have homeless people in the war?'

Taggie pressed her teeth together to prevent her annoyance showing. Questions, questions, always questions. But then she was the older sister, and with that came responsibility. Besides, she was just as nervous as Jem, so she put her arm round her sister's shoulders. 'They must have. So many people lost their homes in the bombing.'

'What *bombing*?' squeaked Jem.

'That's what the Blitz is,' Taggie said in exasperation. 'The German Luftwaffe fly over every night and drop bombs on London. Other cities, too.'

Jemima gave the dark grey sky with its looming barrage balloons a frightened glance. 'People are going to drop bombs on us?'

Taggie desperately wanted to be reassuring, but at the same time she couldn't lie, not to Jem. 'I hope not.' Then she looked round again to check on the leather coat twins. Sure enough, they were there, keeping pace on the other side of the road. The number of pedestrians was thinning out now, which allowed her to see a third leather coat walking fifty paces behind them on their side of the road. 'We're being followed,' she whispered to Jem.

'What!'

'Keep moving.'

'Who is it?'

'I don't know. They look . . . They look like . . .'

'What?'

Taggie pulled a face. 'They look like the kind of spies you see in old films.'

Jemima turned round. 'Oh gosh. Yes, I see what you mean. All four of them are dressed exactly the same.'

'Four?' Taggie gulped. 'Run!'

The sisters ran along the street, drawing far too much attention. A couple of soldiers in uniform called out to them. A few hands made half-hearted attempts to catch their shoulders. Someone even laughed at the sight of two gaudily dressed girls running in a panic.

'Down here,' Taggie said, and they sped off along a

narrow side road. Half a minute later Taggie risked a glance back. The last of the daylight was draining away, and she saw six leather-coated figures silhouetted across the end of the gloomy street. There was no one in front of them. They were in the middle of London, and the whole place seemed deserted.

Felix landed at their feet. The leaden light made his fur seem grey.

'Do you see them?' Taggie shouted as they began to run again.

'Yes, ma'am.' The squirrel scampered alongside, panting. 'They are Ethanu, servants of the Karrak Lords.'

'How did they find us so quickly? How did they know we are here? Taslaf said it wouldn't let anyone follow us.'

'I don't know. But we have to stay ahead of them. Fortunately they can't run like us. Their legs are slow. But they have considerable stamina: they can pursue you for days at a time without rest.'

The three of them pelted along the narrow street and burst out into a broad square with a clump of tall trees in the small central park, surrounded by tall iron railings. It was as deserted as the street behind. Night had come swiftly, reducing the buildings to faint dark outlines.

'Too quick . . .' Taggie murmured. When she paused to take a breath, something made the hairs on her arm prickle, and she instinctively knew the loss of light wasn't natural. The sensation was the same as the one back in the palace garden. This was a shadecast.

She raised her hand, and the coat fell away from her wrist, exposing the charmsward. The bands were already turning of their own accord, and once more the eye symbol was next to the sun symbol. '*Derat al-tooman*,' she called in a clear voice.

A weak twilight broke through the darkness, bathing the square in a cold pink glow. Taggie looked round and gasped. On the other side of the little central park, barely twenty metres away, Lord Golzoth stood behind the railings watching them. Taggie hadn't realized how tall he was before; now she could see he was at least Mr Anatole's height. But so much more intimidating with his eerie cloak that swirled like dense smog as it curled protectively around him. The hood thinned at the front to allow his pale skull-head to emerge, a pair of wrap-around sunglasses were perched on his thin nose with its single nostril.

'Where are you going, little princesses?' the Karrak Lord taunted in a voice which sounded more like a growl.

'Away from you!' Jemima shouted back across the park.

'But *why*?' He sounded genuinely curious.

Taggie let out a grunt of contempt. 'You snatched my father.'

'We brought him back to the Realm which so desperately needs him,' Lord Golzoth said, his voice changing to a smooth croon.

'You're going to kill him,' Taggie snarled.

'Oh, my dear princesses, what lies you have been fed. How awful for you to be brought up on such a diet. But

I'm sure your father believed his lies were good for you. *Were they?*'

'I . . .' Taggie couldn't be disloyal to Dad, no matter how upset she was with him for not telling her about the realms. 'Why did you take him, if not to claim the shell throne for your own? You sent Rannalal knights to kidnap him.'

'They are an honour guard, nothing more. Your father misunderstood. I deeply regret the squabble that ensued at the roundadown. That is why I personally intervened, so that no one would get hurt.'

'You're claiming the shell throne as your own; I know you have your own King. Lord Jothran, who calls himself the King of Night.'

'A caretaker only. My brother stepped in to stop the anarchy which bloomed across the First Realm at the passing of the Queen of Dreams. We simply wish to help. That is why we invited your father to join us. The First Realm needs him. Prince Dino turned his back on everyone when he left, he was ashamed of them and abandoned them. Why do you think he did that?'

'I . . . don't know,' Taggie muttered.

Lord Golzoth's long fingers grasped the park railings, his bejewelled rings glimmering in the soft twilight as he leaned forward and spoke earnestly. 'Your father knows only too well that the First Realm would never change, that it always crushed progress and enlightenment. But now things *are* changing. The Karrak people, my fellow Lords and Ladies, *are* making progress, and we are welcomed by all. We wanted to show your father the hope we have brought. Why, even as we speak he dines in the palace with my brother, Lord Jothran. He sees now the role he must play in the rebirth of the First Realm, and welcomes that. We are joyful, because we need him. We need you as well, sweet princesses. Come. Come with me. *Join us*. Together we can rebuild the First Realm into something worthwhile. Something modern, where all types of people can live together peacefully.'

'Felix?' Jemima whispered. 'Is he right?'

'Pay him no heed, Princess. A Karrak Lord's words are as treacherous as those of any Outer Realm politician,' Felix said with a snarl.

'You would believe someone embittered by his family's curse rather than me?' Lord Golzoth asked in silky surprise.

Felix took a small step forward, his fur bristling as he jumped on to the top of the railings to face the Karrak Lord. 'And why did you curse my family, eh? Can your weasel words explain that away, you deceitful monster.'

'Taggie?' Jemima appealed urgently to her big sister.

Taggie looked round. The six Ethanu appeared, walking steadily down the narrow street behind her. Deep in her mind, memories were stirring. Dark memories of magic used for fighting; powerful magic that could maim and burn and kill. Her ancestors had used such death spells long ago, in terrible wars. These tiny glimpses made Taggie shiver. She didn't want to use such awful things against anyone. Besides, she guessed the Karrak Lord knew some equally vile magic of his own, and would not hesitate to use it against her.

'Come with me,' Lord Golzoth said, his voice now a compelling melody. 'You do not want a life spent in conflict and pain. A union of our great dynasties would bring about a new age of enlightenment across the First Realm. And you are a pretty thing. Lord Jothran would shower such a bride with gifts and wealth. Your life would be lived in unimaginable luxury.' His arm stretched out. And his long fingers seemed so close, as if the park had shrunk to bring him closer to the sisters.

'Eeeuw!' Taggie squealed. 'A bride? I'm twelve! What kind of weirdos are you?' She started searching through other memories the charmsward had opened for her, hunting for something else that might help.

On the other side of the little park, Lord Golzoth let go of the railings, and straightened up. If anything, that made him appear even closer. 'You are weak,' he snapped. The tricky softness of his voice vanished, and he began to growl again. 'Worse than the heretic, Lord Colgath. Such pitiful sentiment is of no use to us. You are in our way, princesses, a pair of scuttling cockroaches to be crushed.'

Golzoth's hands rose up, allowing the swirling smoke cloak to flow back down his long arms. The silver and crystal rings on his strange fingers began to glow with malevolent red light.

Taggie knew that he was gathering a death spell to

strike her with. Her memories were becoming very clear; too many of her ancestors had seen such evil flung at them before. She needed something she could use to deflect Golzoth, and the square was filled with stately old London plane trees. The tree spirits in this Outer Realm were not as quick and lively as those in other Realms, her ancestors remembered, but still, a tree was huge and strong. '*Quazeene*,' she whispered to the trees as her charmsward bands twirled, bringing the earth symbol round with the leaf and arrow. '*Dollfor caroin.*' An enchantment of affection and awakening. Something a Karrak Lord would never use, would never understand.

Golzoth's puzzlement when he heard her words was obvious, even on his skeletal face. He laughed harshly. 'You love plants? Who cares? Weak, stupid, children.' The power of the death spell lit up both of his arms like blue neon signs.

Just then a thick branch came slashing through the twilight above him. It hit him on the side of his swirling cloak with a nasty wallop. Golzoth went flying through the air, shrieking in pain and fury. He landed in a crumpled heap on the road, his smoke cloak billowing wildly around him. Giving a cry of pure anger he clambered to his feet, raising his arms once again.

'Your death pain will last for a century,' he shouted furiously. 'I will see to that.'

Another branch from a different tree came slashing through the air. Golzoth was struck again, sending him

tumbling down the road. He skidded along until he thumped into a wall covered in ivy. The ivy strands writhed like a nest of snakes, coiling round him. Their dark sooty leaves fluttered against his face as if they were angry moths. He spluttered and coughed as he thrashed about, becoming even more entangled. All around the square, trees shook and rustled their leaves as if they were applauding.

'Princess!' Felix said in surprised admiration. 'Well played.'

Taggie glanced over her shoulder at the relentless Ethanu. The six of them had now reached the square. 'Run!' she shouted.

13

ANOTHER PRINCESS

Taggie spotted another street leading off the little square, and headed straight for it. Behind her she could hear Lord Golzoth tearing at the ivy, growling out terrible curses. The Ethanu turned to follow them.

'They're going to kill us,' a terrified Jemima cried.

'We just have to stay ahead,' Taggie reassured her as they sprinted into the new street. The terrace houses on both sides were closed up, their doors shut and their tape-crossed windows dark. 'How did Golzoth find us so quickly?' she asked Felix.

'I don't know,' the white squirrel admitted, as he bounded along the pavement beside them, his tail held parallel to the ground. 'You were right to say Taslaf would never allow him passage. There must be some other Great Gateway of which we know nothing, one who is helping the Karraks. It has allowed them to follow you through time. Karrak Ladies have a reputation as strong seers, they will be searching for you continually now they know you exist.'

Memories flashed through Taggie's brain like a video on fast forward. She tried to think how to cast a charm that would block a seer's sight.

'Oh no,' Jemima cried.

Taggie came to a dead halt, staring through the gloom at the building blocking their way forward. The street was a cul-de-sac, a dead end.

She whirled round. A wave of darkness was creeping along the road towards them, flowing over the pavement and walls beside the Ethanu as they approached at their steady unstoppable pace.

'What do we do, Taggie?' Jemima begged.

Felix drew his sword, its green light shimmering softly along the blade. His teeth chattered in determination, and his tail twitched defiantly upright even though he was just an ordinary-sized squirrel.

The memories in Taggie's mind began to clear. She knew now she would have to cast some of the worst spells her ancestors knew. It was a dreadful thing, but she didn't have a choice. Besides, somehow she didn't feel too bad about slaying the Ethanu. However, behind them would be Golzoth, and that would be a very different fight.

An engine's heavy grumbling grew louder just as Taggie prepared herself to utter the harsh words of a death spell. Then suddenly a pair of narrow headlight beams were cutting through the dark shadows that swamped the cul-de-sac. They flashed across the six Ethanu, who turned in surprise.

Brakes squealed, and the engine thrummed. Taggie and Jemima held their hands across their eyes, trying to see past the glare. It was some kind of big truck jammed into the end of the cul-de-sac.

One of the Ethanu hooted in its own language. There was a violet flash. It showed Taggie a small woman in a khaki army uniform standing beside the truck. She was surrounded by a ball of fading violet light as it withered into the tarmac without touching her. When the last of the flickers had dwindled away, she pointed a rod at the Ethanu and yelled: '*Korruth'tu*.'

The rod began to spit out tiny globes of sharp blue flame as if it was some kind of machine gun. A deafening crackling filled the cul-de-sac. Some of the blue flames *zinged* through the air just above Taggie's head. She and Jemima dived for the ground, covering their ears against the hideous sound.

Abruptly it was quiet again. The shadecast was broken, and the cul-de-sac was fully illuminated by the truck's headlights. Taggie raised her head. All six Ethanu were lying on the ground, their leather coats smoking.

The woman in the army uniform was walking towards them. She was quite young, Taggie saw, probably still a teenager; with dark curly hair sticking out from the edge of her peaked cap. And she had a lovely welcoming smile. 'Hello there,' she said in a very posh voice. 'That was a close call. You chaps are lucky David called me. These Ethanu are beastly difficult to track down. One is always on the look-out for them.'

'D-David?' Taggie mumbled in a daze.

'The jeweller. He doesn't often see coins from the First Realm. So when he does, he knows there's some kind of shenanigans afoot.'

'Please . . . who are you?' Jemima asked.

The woman stuck her hand out for Taggie to shake. 'Subaltern Elizabeth Windsor of the Auxiliary Territorial Service. But that's just my cover, I've actually been raised to the Grand Order of Mage Knights. Jolly nice to meet you.'

Taggie let out a groan of shock as she realized who their rescuer was. 'You're Princess Elizabeth,' she exclaimed.

'Huh?' Jemima grunted. 'You mean, she's—'

'Yes!' Taggie interrupted, hopefully stopping Jemima from saying anything too stupid.

'And who are you chaps, exactly?' Princess Elizabeth asked with a wink.

'Taggie Paganuzzi. Er, actually, I'm a princess, too. Of the First Realm. And so's my sister Jemima. We're just totally honoured to meet you, ma'am.'

'Poor Papa is frightfully busy fighting the rathwai most nights,' Princess Elizabeth told the sisters. They were all perched on the worn seats of her big army truck, bouncing their way along London's half-empty streets.

'What are *they*?' Jemima asked. She hadn't stopped staring admiringly at Princess Elizabeth since they climbed into the cab.

'Rathwai are the Karrak Lords' air beasts, as big as

elephants, with talons like swords and razor-sharp beaks stronger than a crocodile's mouth. The diabolical things fly in with the Luftwaffe bombers; they cause so much damage, and then carry off children from the houses they smash up. Thankfully some olri-gi have offered to help us. Papa and the Knights of the Black Garter ride on them to fight off the rathwai. It's so desperately hard, one worries terribly about him.'

'Olri-gi?' Jemima asked faintly.

Princess Elizabeth grinned. 'Dragons, to you and me. But don't ever call them that to their faces – they're dreadfully quick to take offence, it's like *them* calling *us* sacks of meat.'

'There are dra— . . . olri-gi here, in the Outer Realm?' squeaked Taggie.

'Only while the war's on, obviously,' chattered Princess Elizabeth, oblivious to the sisters' shocked faces. 'They live in the Realm of Air normally. But wherever the Karraks come to spread their evil, good eggs band together to help one another.'

'Thank you again for helping us,' Taggie said. She was still trying to get used to the idea that dragons were flying over London as part of the Battle of Britain – and that people rode on them! It was strangely wonderful.

'Always happy to help a Paganuzzi,' Princess Elizabeth said. 'But I am surprised we haven't met before. I did visit the Queen of Dreams' palace a couple of years ago, which was jolly lovely. She never mentioned any princesses. There was only her son, Prince Dino. He's a funny little chap, quite mad about football, don't you know. I promised I'd take him to a game at Wembley after the war is over.'

'We're not from this time, really,' Taggie said cautiously.

'Oh really . . . those wretched Great Gateways,' Princess Elizabeth said. 'Sometimes I think they're more trouble than they're worth.'

'You might be right,' Taggie agreed. 'So you know about the Realms?'

'Of course I do. One's family is one of the anointed guardians of the Great Gateways in this Realm. Most of the Outer Realm's original royal families are descended from the elder mages who forged the Great Gateways. So when the Dark Lords and Ladies began to emerge from Mirlyn's Gate we led the fight against them. Papa still does, along with various cousins and a few knights with some magic lore. But there are so few of us these days.'

'That must be hard for you.'

'It is one's duty and destiny,' Princess Elizabeth said proudly. 'What about you? The Paganuzzi line has many obligations, I know.'

'So it would seem,' Taggie said with a sigh. 'And to carry them out I need to get back to my proper time, which is your future. Could you drop us off at King's Cross station, please? We'll catch a train to Grantham.'

'You'll be wanting to use the Arasath Gateway at Orchard Cottage, then?'

'Yes. It can undo the damage it's done. I think. I hope.' After everything that had just happened, Taggie didn't want to think of what awaited her. She felt safe riding in the truck with Princess Elizabeth; it was a precious time where she could relax in peace.

'I think it's best if I drive you back to Orchard Cottage myself,' Princess Elizabeth said with a friendly smile. 'That horrible Karrak Lord is still on the loose. He must want you very badly to summon so many Ethanu. They normally creep about, spying and sabotaging the war effort. To lose so many in one night will enrage the Karraks in Berlin.'

'Will we be safe travelling with you?' Jemima asked urgently.

Princess Elizabeth patted the rod that was lying across her lap. 'Nobody crosses a Mage Knight carrying a loaded sceptre. Not if they jolly well know what's good for them.'

'Is that what that is?' Jemima asked. The rod had been carved from dark oak a very long time ago. One end bulged slightly, where it was inset with a trio of small blue jewels that glimmered from an internal light, as if each caged a star.

'Yes,' Princess Elizabeth said. 'That gaudy thing, the Royal Sceptre, with all the big jewels which they keep in the Tower of London, is just for show. It's worth so much money people think it's tremendously important. Whereas this old beauty is a real one. One's family has wielded them for many centuries. Legend says King Edmund Ironside brought them back after the Battle of Rothgarnal, where they'd been fashioned for him by Second Realm battle mages.'

'What's it like?' a fascinated Jemima asked. 'The Second Realm, I mean?'

'Hot and dry,' Felix said curtly.

'Do the Karraks appear often in this realm?' Taggie asked.

'No, thank Heavens,' Princess Elizabeth said. 'But see what happens when they do. The Karraks are the true power behind the Nazis, and now they're sweeping through Europe, expanding their dominion in this Realm. Didn't you think it was strange that a whole country would suddenly embrace such an evil? There are dark enchantments at work at the heart of Europe, let me tell you.'

'I see,' Taggie said. 'I didn't know. But then I only

found out that I'm going to inherit the First Realm's shell throne a day ago.'

Princess Elizabeth gave her a sympathetic look. 'Poor you.'

The drive up to Melham took hours. Taggie, who had driven up the A1 countless times in the back of her mother's big comfortable car, watching a film on the seatback screens while they raced along way above the speed limit, was appalled by how narrow and potholed the road was. They didn't have dual carriageways in the 1940s, or safety barriers. Wartime also meant that their headlights were reduced to thin beams that really didn't reveal very much, and it was a dark night.

Taggie suspected Princess Elizabeth was using some kind of charm to see ahead – Felix certainly didn't seem bothered by the journey – so she spent a lot of the time trying to get used to the charmsward and all the knowledge it remembered for her. Somewhere around Stevenage she thought she finally managed to weave a wardveil around herself, which should make her invisible to whatever Karrak Lady seers were tracking her. By the time they were passing through Stamford she'd sorted out the various shield invocations, which could defend her against Karrak death spells. It wasn't much, but it made her feel a little more confident about the task ahead.

Midnight had long passed by the time the truck rolled into Melham. Taggie and Jemima weren't entirely surprised to see the village was almost the same in the 1940s as it was in the twenty-first century.

'Thank you, ma'am,' Taggie said as the truck stopped just down the road from Orchard Cottage.

'You're welcome,' Princess Elizabeth said kindly. 'And jolly good luck on your quest.'

'I'm sorry we couldn't tell you why we're here,' Taggie said. 'But the Queen of Dreams said fate and destiny cannot be altered.'

'She's quite right,' Princess Elizabeth said.

'Goodbye,' Jemima said with a huge smile. 'Please don't forget us. Please!'

'Crikey, I'm not going to do that, not after all tonight's excitement. If you can, do come and visit me at Buckingham Palace when everything gets back to normal.'

'Oh yes!' Jemima gushed enthusiastically. 'We'd love to.'

'Be firm with the Great Gateway,' Princess Elizabeth told Taggie with a twinkle in her eye. 'Let it jolly well know who's in charge.'

'I will. I promise.'

'See you soon.'

And with that, Princess Elizabeth revved the truck's big engine, and drove off into the night.

Taggie and Jemima and Felix crept through the gardens towards the orchard. There were no lights on in Orchard Cottage. Taggie wasn't sure which distant relatives lived in the place during the war, and didn't particularly want to find out. Whoever they were, they kept the gardens a lot smarter than Dad ever did.

There was an ordinary gate in the fuchsia hedge between the garden and the orchard. They went through to find perfectly pruned trees in neat rows.

'Can you see any gnomes?' an anxious Jemima asked Felix.

The squirrel was perched on top of the gate, searching the orchard with his purple glasses. 'No, it's clear.'

'When this is all over and we get back, I'm going to sort out the garden and orchard,' Taggie decided. 'It looks much nicer like this.'

'A pleasing thought, Princess,' Felix said, he raced along the grass, no more than a small grey shadow.

'Dad likes it all shaggy,' Jemima said.

'Dad needs to change.'

'Taggie!'

'Well he does.' Taggie stopped in the middle of the mown strip of grass, and put her hands on her hips. 'He should have told us about the Realms.'

Felix shot up an apple tree and gripped one of the lower branches to look down at the sisters. 'He was being a good father,' he said. 'He wanted you to enjoy your childhood.'

'Ha!' Taggie waved her arms exuberantly. 'Do I look like I'm enjoying myself?'

'Stop being so cross with Daddy,' Jemima said. 'It's horrible. He's in trouble.'

Taggie gave her sister a glare – which was completely wasted in the darkness. 'Well, he wouldn't be in trouble if he'd stayed in the First Realm like he was supposed to, and sat on the shell throne when Grandma died.'

'If he hadn't travelled to this Realm he would never have met your mother,' Felix said quietly. 'You would not have been born.'

The darkness didn't hide Jemima's expression of satisfaction.

'I know,' Taggie whispered, and all her anger withered away like roses in winter. But there was something else bothering her about Dad. 'This is the nineteen forties, isn't it?' she asked.

'Yes, ma'am,' Felix said.

'And right now Dad is a boy?'

'Yes,' Felix agreed from his apple tree.

'But in our time he's only forty-seven. Remember, Jem, we got him a birthday cake and everything last year. That's in about seventy years' time. So how can that be?'

'Your family ages slowly,' Felix said solemnly. 'All those descended from mages grow to a great age. Providing they don't go and get themselves killed doing stupid things. I suspect your father was speaking falsely about his age so he could appear more normal to the people of this Realm.'

'How old do squirrels get?' Jemima asked brightly.

'I couldn't say.'

'Lord Golzoth said your family were cursed,' Taggie said.

'He is correct.'

'What curse?' Jemima asked.

The squirrel gave her a very surprised look. His forepaw swept down his front. 'We were not always like this, ma'am.'

'Oh,' an embarrassed Jemima muttered. 'What did you look like, then? Before, I mean?'

'Jem!'

'Nothing you need concern yourself with.' Felix said quietly. 'Now we must concentrate on helping your father.'

'But—'

'We need to get to Arasath,' Felix announced firmly.

The sisters headed towards the far end of the orchard, with Felix running along branches overhead and jumping between trees.

When thcy found the dark stone circle set in the ground, Taggie looked down into the hole feeling a strange sense of eagerness. Arasath was at the bottom, and she was confident enough now to know that this time she'd be getting some answers.

'I'll do this,' she said, because she remembered exactly what charm opened the roundadown. There were a lot of tiny periwinkles growing amid the thick grass at the top. She plucked one of the tiny blue and white flowers, dropping it into the hole. '*Zarek fol*,' she said calmly.

The first stone rumbled as it slid out of the side of

the roundadown. Then the second stone emerged just below it.

'Crikey, Taggie,' an impressed Jemima gasped. 'You're getting good at magic.'

Taggie smiled a little smugly and took the torch out of her pocket. She started to walk down the emerging stone steps.

As before, the bottom of the roundadown was dry and warm, with a springy layer of leaves. Taggie stood straight-backed, facing the door that had no handle, with Felix on one side and Jemima on the other. 'I am Taggie, Princess of the First Realm, and its future Queen. You will open to the time where I belong and take me home.'

'You have grown, Majesty,' Arasath's solemn voice said behind her.

Taggie didn't flinch or try to look over her shoulder; instead she narrowed her eyes and focused on the iron-bound planks of the door ahead. 'Why did you do that? Why did you deceive me?'

'I opened to a First Realm you needed to understand, a First Realm you needed to connect to. And love. I did it for love. For love is important above all things. Love is how you will triumph, Princess Taggie.'

'Oh,' she said, slightly flustered. 'That's all very well, but we've been chased by Ethanu, and nearly killed by Lord Golzoth. Why did you let him follow us?'

'I did not,' Arasath said.

'You did!' Jemima blurted.

Taggie squeezed her sister's hand. 'Then how did he wind up in the middle of the Second World War with us?' she asked Arasath.

'Some other Gateway opened here for him.'

'Which one?'

'I don't know.'

'So you can't help, then?'

'I am but an opening. I have some choice over who or what passes through me, but apart from that I play no part in the lives of those who live in the Realms.'

'But you chose to show me that moment in history,' Taggie said shrewdly. 'Why?'

'It could have been any moment,' Arasath replied.

Taggie grinned. That was an evasive answer. It could have been any moment but it wasn't; she'd seen her father, her grandmother and Princess Elizabeth. That wasn't chance, a random day. Just by understanding that, she felt as if she'd won an argument. 'You do take part,' she told the devious Great Gateway. 'And one day, I'll find out why, and what it is you're doing.'

'Whatever will be will be.'

'Then let me go back to the First Realm, the one of my own time.'

'Majesty,' Arasath said respectfully. The door in front of Taggie swung open silently. 'Welcome home. Though sadly you may find your home is not welcoming.'

'It will be,' Taggie told the Great Gateway.

Determination carried her along the long curving

brick tunnel. Determination kept her legs steady and her confidence high. Then they rounded the last curve and came to the entrance.

Taggie, Jemima and Felix looked out into the First Realm. All Taggie wanted was to see the reassuring sight of the lush green curving land, with sparkling seas above her, the bright little sun shining warmly in the midst of it all.

'Oh no!' Taggie gasped in dismay. She thought she might cry at the awful sight before her.

14

THE REALM OF THE KING OF NIGHT

At first Taggie thought she was looking at a gigantic grey wall encircling the Great Gateway's entrance. Then, as her eyes got used to the miserable light, she saw that the First Realm was besieged by snowstorms. Thick swirls of ugly grey cloud crawled across the land in every direction. The beautiful quilt of green fields and forests she'd seen on her last visit were locked in a hard frost, with flurries of snow swirling between deep drifts.

When she lifted her head to see the sun that hung in the centre of the First Realm it was hidden behind a veil of mooncloud from which the cheerful colours had drained away. The clouds too were now sickly grey, and thickening. Vast night shadows smothered the ground below them, their edges growing even as she watched. It wouldn't be long, Taggie realized, before all the nights merged together, leaving the Realm in permanent darkness.

'What has happened here?' she wailed.

'The Karraks have brought darkness and despair to this realm,' Felix said sadly. 'This is fast becoming a realm where their own kind can laugh at our misery and flourish.'

'This is dreadful,' she said, aghast. 'I never imagined

anything so bad. What can I ever do to put it right?'

Felix's paw took her hand. The white squirrel was almost her height again, and his black eyes held a warm glimmer of kindness. 'Your own question shows your character. You ask what you *can* do: who but a selfless person would ask that when confronted with such wickedness? Take courage – no one is asking you to fight this alone. Knowing you live and have come home will bring hope to the whole First Realm. With hope, anything can be achieved.'

Jemima flung her arms round her sister. 'It's OK, Taggie, it's OK. Really it is. We'll find Daddy and he'll know what to do.'

Taggie wiped her hand across her eyes. 'Thanks, Jem. You're right, we came here to rescue Dad, and that's what we'll do.' She looked at the forlorn winter landscape and shuddered at the damage that had befallen such a sweet realm. 'But we'll need help. Where can we find help, Felix?'

'There will be people, ma'am; the old palace guard, the sheriffs and rangers, ordinary folk with a stout heart. Many took to the woods and caves when the sky grew cold and the moonclouds turned against us. They harass the minions of the Karrak Lords and Ladies as best they can. I'm sure we can find them.'

'All right then,' Taggie said and rose to her feet. 'You know, Jem, I can feel them, all our ancestors, they're happy we're here. And we will find a way to deal with Jothran. We will. I swear it.'

*

Taggie, Jemima and Felix walked down the path towards the canal station building. With the snow already over half a metre deep, they only knew where the path lay from the tracks of others, whose boots and shoes had tramped it down.

'Rannalal knights,' Felix said after he'd examined the tracks. 'Among others.'

'The ones who captured Dad?' Taggie asked.

'Very likely, Princess.'

'Who else has come this way?'

'I don't know. Several men. Definitely a horse, I expect that was Lord Golzoth: the hoofprints are deep.'

'I'm scared of him,' Jemima said. 'I'm sorry, I know princesses are supposed to be brave and noble and stuff, but he's just so horrible, and he wants to kill us.'

'You are wise to be so cautious, ma'am,' Felix said. 'Only a fool underestimates their enemies, especially one as powerful as Lord Golzoth.'

'Felix,' Jemima said in a tired voice. 'I know I'm a princess now and everything, but please will you stop calling me *ma'am*?'

Felix dipped his head. 'As you wish, er . . .'

'My friends call me Jem.'

'Jem.'

'Thank you.'

The canal was frozen over. Big icicles hung from the edge of the station's platform canopy. And there was someone sitting on one of the benches underneath.

At first they thought it was just a big bundle of rags. Then Taggie noticed the gold threads peeping out from under the frost which had settled in all the fabric's creases.

'Mr Anatole?' she asked in surprise.

The figure didn't move. Taggie bent down and slowly pushed the fur-lined hood away from his red face. He was breathing very slowly. Little flakes of snow had settled on his nose and eyelashes.

'Mr Anatole, it's me, Taggie. Taggie Paganuzzi. We met at Orchard Cottage, remember?'

The eyes slowly opened. 'You see me again, my lady,' he said forlornly, so very different to the tall man she'd met in the lounge of Orchard Cottage. Then, dressed in his splendid robes, he'd possessed a confidence and determination which were sorely lacking now. Even sitting down he seemed stooped and weakened, while his fine cloth robes under the dusting of snow had become dull and poor.

'Yes, I see you,' Taggie assured him.

'I thought nobody saw me. I sat here and cast a shade when they dragged Prince Dino away. There was nothing I could do. Not against a company of Rannalal and Ethanu and a Karrak Lord. I am a scholar not a soldier. So I watched them go on their way and wept for our lost realm. And I waited.'

'Waited for what?' Jemima asked.

'A miracle. This seemed as good a place as any. And now

here you are. The princesses we never knew. A rightful heir to the shell throne. A miracle indeed.'

Taggie smiled gently at the old man. 'I'm not a miracle, Mr Anatole. I'm here to get my father back. After that we'll see what can be done for the First Realm. Can you help? I know you helped my grandmother, Felix said you were her adviser.'

Mr Anatole gave her a small admiring smile, his white teeth bright in his dark red face. 'Something like that, yes. I will always serve the Queen of Dreams if she asks, no matter who she is. And now it would seem you are our Queen-to-be. Without you, my lady, we are nothing.'

'Come on then,' Taggie said, and held out her hand. 'Let's find people who'll help. There have to be some, somewhere.'

Mr Anatole took her hand and rose slowly, his stiff joints causing him great difficulty.

'Aren't you cold?' Jemima asked. She'd pulled her colourful bobble hat down tight over her ears, and jammed her gloved hands into her pockets – and she still felt cold.

'No,' Mr Anatole said. 'We Shadarain do not suffer from cold nor heat as your kind do.'

'Lucky you,' Jemima grumbled.

'We'd better move,' Felix said, watching the snowy landscape alertly. 'The Karraks have patrols out. I don't want to be caught on open ground, not in snow. We can't run through snow.'

Mr Anatole peered round into grey gloom. 'The town

129

of Charavik lies that way along the canal. It was home to the Dolvoki Rangers, who are tough people, loyal to the Queen of Dreams. I expect they've taken to the Farndorn Forest that covers these hills. Not even an army of Karraks could find them in the Farndorn.'

'Then how will we?' Jemima asked.

Mr Anatole smiled, which dislodged the last of the snow clinging to his face. 'We don't have to. They will find us.'

It was a long arduous trek over the snow-covered meadows and streams to the dense woodland beyond. As it dragged on, Taggie became conscious of how bright her orange coat was. How easy to see in a world gone grey.

The hills grew steadily taller as they edged their way closer. Legs grew tired at kicking through so much pristine snow. Mr Anatole insisted on taking the lead as they went up one of the foothills, flattening down as much as he could with his boots so the sisters could traipse along behind him. Felix scampered along effortlessly at their side, yet despite his size his hind paws barely left a dint in the fluffy snow.

'Mr Anatole, where did the Dark Lords and Ladies come from?' Taggie asked.

'Ah,' Mr Anatole sighed. 'That is a story of the mages from the First Times: it was both their biggest triumph and greatest disaster. At the start of the First Times, when the angels brought people to the Realms, magic was wild and strong, flowing through every rock and stream. Some people grew very skilled at shaping it. Spells, we call such shapes now, though they are small weak things compared to how it was back then. Those who had the greatest skills became the mages whose names still carry through history. The most powerful seers of those times saw other Realms beyond their own, and even learned to talk with their fellows across the grand divide. Once that talk began they formed the illustrious Universal Fellowship of Mages, with Mirlyn, the most powerful mage of all, as their leader.'

'Yes,' Taggie said enthusiastically. 'Felix mentioned them, and Arasath spoke of the Fellowship as if they still existed.' She enjoyed hearing about the First Realm's history; if only lessons at school were half as fascinating.

'In a way the Fellowship does still exist,' Mr Anatole said. 'For over a hundred years they devoted themselves and their families to finding a way that would allow them to physically pass between the Realms. Eventually, they tamed the last of the wild magic and used it to forge what are now called the Great Gateways.'

'So how many Great Gateways are there?' Taggie asked.

'No one is certain,' Mr Anatole said. 'For some closed up over time as they grew tired of their own existence, and these now sleep eternity away. You see, each one contains the essence of a Fellowship mage. Only the will of a mage so powerful could shape and control such wild magic. Such a soul is the foundation of a Great Gateway, and also its keeper.'

'The Great Gateways are alive, then?'

'After a fashion, yes. Though they perform no other task than that which they were forged to do.'

'Hmm,' Taggie said sceptically. After talking to Arasath she had her own suspicions about that. 'Why did the mages do it?' she asked.

'Some say it was to become immortal. Though such a life comes with a terrible price, you remain one thing in one place forever, with only travellers to talk to. Some speculate that is why the Great Gateways are becoming increasingly difficult with the peoples of the Realms – there is certainly less traffic through them than there used to be, even in my grandfather's time. And there were always restrictions on travel to the Outer Realm. However, legend says that the Universal Fellowship mages were utterly selfless, and went about their task so they might grant the most extraordinary boon to their descendants. And one can understand why so many believe that. The Great Gateways were such a magnificent gift to the Realms: they allowed trade and travel which enriched everyone.'

'And one got opened into a dark Realm by mistake?'

'No,' Mr Anatole said unhappily. 'It was not a Realm, and certainly not by mistake. Mirlyn was said to be left desolate after the Great Gateways into the Outer Realm were opened, for then there was nowhere else left to go. He was the only Universal Fellowship mage not to forge himself into a gateway. Instead, he toiled on by himself – some say growing madder and madder – until he finally found a new frontier to reach out to. With his triumph complete, he forged himself into the greatest and most powerful gateway of all, reaching further than anyone had dared dream, extending far beyond our Realms into another universe entirely. Our universe is one which is ultimately built of light. Mirlyn's Gate opens to a universe built upon the dark, the opposite of everything we are.'

'So that's where the Karrak Lords and Ladies come from . . .' Taggie breathed in fascination.

'Yes. The result of Mirlyn's Gate opening has been catastrophic. Peoples from this universe who went through tried to change what they found, for it was so monstrous to their eyes. Meanwhile, the dark creatures who travelled this way seek to do the same here, because everything they find is wrong for them. It is a conflict which cannot

end, for there is no common ground – we are intrinsically opposed.'

Taggie turned round. 'Jem, do you think we could—' She broke off and gave her sister a suspicious stare. 'Jem!'

'Huh? Yes?'

'Are you listening to your iPod?'

Jemima plucked earplugs out from under her striped bobble hat. 'What?'

'Oh, Jem! This is important.'

'What is?'

'Jem! Come on, you have to pay attention to what's going on. We're all alone here, and Felix and Mr Anatole aren't even sure this is the right route. You must start—'

'It *is*.'

'It is what?'

'The right route. That's the way.' Jemima pointed across to a fold in the land, which formed the start of a narrow valley that cut back into the hills. 'Almost, anyway. We should go into the trees down there.'

Taggie gave her sister an infuriated look. 'What are you talking about?'

Jemima stared back, equally stubborn. 'That's the right route to take. I know it is.'

Taggie liked the idea of heading back down a slope again. But the trees up ahead were a lot closer now. 'Don't be stupid, you can't know that.'

Jemima's hands clenched into tough little fists, which she jabbed into her sides. 'That *is* the right way.

And that's the way I'm going. So there.'

'Princess,' Mr Anatole said quietly to Taggie. 'Perhaps we should consider what your sister said.'

Taggie couldn't believe he was taking Jemima's side. Jemima who had *that* smirk growing on her face.

'My sister is a pain,' she told him, because clearly Mr Anatole needed to be warned about Jemima's annoying nature. 'She doesn't know anything.'

'And yet,' Felix said, 'only two days ago you had never seen a talking squirrel, nor fought off a Karrak Lord with magic. Jemima is also a princess; the Blossom Princess in fact, descended from Usrith, as are you.'

'See!' Jemima said triumphantly. 'Er . . . what's a Blossom Princess?'

'Traditionally,' Mr Anatole said. 'Any sister of the Queen of Dreams is referred—'

'Someone's coming,' Taggie interrupted. She pointed back along the track they'd left across the snow-shrouded meadows. About half a mile away, dark red shapes were moving surprisingly quickly towards them. 'Oh no, they look like . . .'

'Rannalal,' Felix confirmed. 'A whole company of them. They're mounted on usrogs, too.'

'What are—? Oh never mind,' Taggie said. From the way Felix's paws were jittering, she knew the answer wouldn't be good.

'Hurry now!' Felix said. 'We don't have much time.'

15

BATTLE AT THE FROZEN WATERFALL

Taggie and Jemima ran through the rumpled snow just behind Mr Anatole, whose long strides carried him along comfortably. Perhaps *too* comfortably: after only a minute the sisters were panting heavily as they struggled to keep up. Taggie had thought trudging up the snow-covered slope before was tough. This was ten times worse. The treeline was at least half a mile ahead, and the slope was getting steeper all the time.

Behind them the short, armoured Rannalal were catching up fast. The usrogs they rode resembled a cross between spiders and wild boars, with eight legs scampering easily over the snow. Nasty, eager squeals came from jaws with sharp, upward curving tusks.

'We're not going to make it,' Taggie gasped.

'Taggie, please, I know we have to go down there,' Jemima pleaded.

Taggie glanced across the slope to the little valley. It was downhill at least, but the trees at the bottom were even further away than those ahead.

'Jem—'

'Please. Taggie, I *know* that's the way. I truly do.'

Her sister was telling the truth – Taggie was suddenly certain of it. Jemima was annoying in many ways, but still they were sisters, and Taggie knew her better than anyone. But they'd surely never reach the trees before the Rannalal caught them. Not by running. 'Mr Anatole,' she shouted. 'Head for that tree.'

The tall Shadarain altered direction, powering through the cloying snow towards the tree Taggie had seen up ahead. It was one of several growing in the undulating meadows that led up the forest. An ancient beech which had already lost several boughs to age and wind.

Taggie barely saw it now; her mind teemed with fleeting memories as she sought the kind of spell she needed. As they drew near she raised her arm. The symbols on the charmsward bands glowed with the green light of spring leaves as they spun round: a lightning bolt flicked up next to wind, which in turn settled against an axe. Not quite a death spell, and she needed to apply the magic just so . . . '*Milsoa. Toisi.*'

A pale wedge of pink light shot out of her palm, slicing into the tree. It quivered, and a long oval sheet of wood peeled off the trunk.

'*Milsoa. Toisi,*' she repeated.

Another big oval fell to the ground beside the first.

'What are you doing?' Jemima demanded.

Taggie gave her a wild grin. 'We need to get down fast, don't we?'

Jemima suddenly realized what the ovals of wood were

for, and laughed in shock. 'Oh yes. Yes!'

'Get on,' Taggie told Jemima as they arrived at the tree. The mounted Rannalal knights were barely a hundred metres behind now. She could make out their stumpy legs beating the sides of the usrogs, four heels jabbing in, urging their horrible spider-beasts to run faster.

Jemima jumped on to the oval and clung grimly to the edges. Taggie pushed it with all her strength and it began to slide over the snow. After that fierce first push the makeshift sledge moved easily, starting to pick up speed as they headed down the slope. Taggie managed another five paces before she leaped on. The sledge skidded along by itself now, accelerating fast. She saw Felix standing on the front of the other piece of wood as Mr Anatole pushed him along. Then the old royal adviser was jumping on.

A couple of arrows whistled down behind them as the Rannalal realized they were about to loose their quarry. But they didn't have the range.

Jemima was laughing so loud she almost choked. 'Brilliant, Taggie. Just brilliant!'

And still they were accelerating. Taggie saw a startled sheep lumbering out of the way, and chortled happily.

'Taggie!' Jemima screeched.

There was a hawthorn hedge directly ahead of them.

'*Droiak!*' Taggie yelled instinctively, very pleased she'd spent all that time in the army truck rehearsing such things. Out of her hand flashed a small bluish lightning bolt, which she only just managed to line up in time. A big section of the hedge disintegrated in a shower of sparkling embers and steaming chunks of snow.

The sisters hurtled through the gap, clinging to one another. Then laughed hysterically as they were through. Taggie checked to see where Felix and Mr Anatole were, and if she'd have to blow up another bit of hedge for them with the destruction spell (which she quite fancied doing). But they managed to steer through the smouldering gap.

The crude sledge continued to streak along its downward path. Taggie watched the Rannalal start off after them, their usrogs kicking up plumes of powdery snow as they cantered forward. They weren't going to give up, she realized. That cooled her sense of excitement more than the icy air striking her face. Ever since Lord Golzoth had pulled her dad down into the depths of the roundadown, it seemed like she'd done nothing but run away from the Karrak Lords and their followers.

The death spells lurked at the back of her mind like hornets asleep in their nest. It would be so easy to unleash them. But killing would make her no different than the Karraks. 'Not unless I have no choice,' she promised herself.

They reached the bottom of the slope, where it levelled out to take them to the bank of the frozen stream. The wooden oval skidded to a stop amid the ice-crusted reeds which lined the bank.

'This really *is* the way,' Jemima said meekly. 'I don't know how I know, but I'm sure about it.'

'I trust you, Jem,' Taggie said with a quick, warm smile.

Mr Anatole and Felix arrived in a swoosh of ice particles. 'Well played again, Princess,' Felix said.

Mr Anatole climbed off his sledge and gave Taggie a respectful bow. 'Majesty, your magic is stronger than any I've witnessed before.'

Taggie held up her arm, showing him the charmsward. 'It's my ancestors who show me what to do,' she explained.

'Yes, Majesty . . .' Something in the old man's voice betrayed doubt.

'Come,' Felix said. 'The Rannalal are upon us still. We should be able to lose the brutes in the forest.'

Taggie wasn't so sure. Nonetheless she followed the big white squirrel as he bounded along the flat surface of the frozen stream. Behind them, the company of mounted Rannalal were halfway down the slope.

'I'll do what I have to,' Taggie reassured her friends. 'If they do catch up with us, they'll be sorry.'

The edge of the Farndorn Forest was just a few yards away now; a thick dark wall of big gnarled trunks that opened around the stream to form a cave entrance. Ropes of ivy and honeysuckle that were covered in a thick crust of frost dangled down like a curtain, obscuring whatever was on the other side. If indeed there was anything.

Taggie murmured the incantation for a shield which coiled invisibly round her. Prepared thus, she brushed the frigid white cords aside and hurried in.

The stream wound onward through the trees. Giant

oaks and pines and beech and ash and chestnuts lined the side of the stream, producing a wonderful shaggy white avenue. A few meagre shafts of light cut through the gloom to dapple the ground.

Then the trees parted, and the stream opened out into a broad pond with a rock wall on the far side. A frozen waterfall formed a jagged staircase up to the higher ground beyond.

'We'll have to go around,' Taggie said. She didn't think even Felix could clamber up that ice-slicked rock.

Just then a red streak shot down from the roof of leaves and branches above the pond. Taggie found herself looking at the tip of an arrow that glimmered with the unpleasant violet of bad magic. The arrow was notched in a bow. The bow was held by a skymaid in a dark grey leather tunic that blended in perfectly with the winter forest. She was young, no more than Taggie's age, with long ginger hair that floated round her head as if the strands weighed nothing. Big wings blurred the air behind her.

'Stop right there, foul Karrak creature,' she proclaimed fiercely. 'Or I will send you back to whatever hell realm you came from.'

'Whoa!' Taggie exclaimed in surprise. 'Hey, I'm not a Karrak.' She tugged her hood off and gave the skymaid a desperate look. 'See? Actually . . .' She faltered slightly. 'I'm a princess. I'm the heir to the shell throne.'

'And I'm a racing skyhog,' the red-haired skymaid scoffed. Laughter echoed round the pool's clearing. That was when Taggie noticed the other skymaids and skyboys hovering above the pond – over a dozen of them, and each one with a bow that held an arrow ready.

'She really *is* a princess,' Jemima squeaked indignantly. 'So just do as you're told.'

The skymaid pulled her bowstring back a fraction, as if she'd been challenged.

'Not helping,' Taggie grunted to her sister from the corner of her mouth. 'Look, I'm going to show you something, so don't shoot, OK?' She slowly raised her arm, and the coat sleeve fell down to reveal the charmsward with every symbol shining bright emerald and the bands slowly turning.

The red-haired skymaid frowned, lowering her bow a fraction, and peering round the violet arrowhead. 'That is one of this realm's crown jewels; it belonged to the Queen of Dreams, may she rest in peace.'

'Yes! She was my grandmother.'

'Young lady,' Mr Anatole said in a loud, commanding voice. 'Lower your weapon, please. You address your Queen-to-be.'

'A Queen?' the skymaid asked. 'We are to have a Queen of Dreams again? How can such a thing be so? The only prince we had abandoned this realm long ago.'

'Not any more,' Taggie said. 'That's the reason we're here. My father, Prince Dino, has been captured by the Karrak Lords. We've come to rescue him.'

'Is this true?'

'Perfectly true,' Felix said.

The skymaid's bow lowered as she peered at the squirrel. 'A Weldowen,' she exclaimed. 'This is an odd day.'

'You're telling me,' Taggie muttered. She heard a commotion behind her, and started. 'The Rannalal are coming. They're chasing us. Please, will you help?'

The skymaid's grin was wide and generous. 'I am Sophie, lady-in-waiting to my flock,' the skymaid said. 'And I am truly pleased to meet you, Queen-to-be.'

'Please call me Taggie. And the Rannalal knights . . . ?'

'Cousins!' Sophie bellowed. 'Get down here.'

Four of the skymaids swooped down. Two of them caught Taggie under her arms and bore her aloft.

'I'm Tilly,' said the one with short blonde hair.

'And I'm Elsie,' the other informed her, the one with pale red hair that would have reached down to her knees if it had ever been calm enough. 'A skymaid no more, but a skyhuntress, now! We're going to burn every one of the dark creatures from our Realm.'

'Right,' Taggie said meekly. 'OK.'

'Elsie, calm down,' Tilly said, with a grin for Taggie.

They set her down atop the frozen waterfall, and shot off up into the air, wings blurring. Jemima was put down beside her by Sophie's other two skymaid cousins. They saluted Taggie with their bows, and darted up into the tangle of branches and crisp-frosted leaves above the pond, shimmering from sight.

Taggie crouched down and peered over the rocks.

Felix had vanished, and Mr Anatole was hurrying into the bushes where he could conceal himself.

A few moments later the company of Rannalal came charging on to the frozen pond. They reined in their usrogs, and looked about for their prey.

Sophie plummeted out of the sky to hover right in front of the company commander, a nocked arrow inches from his blood-red helmet, its glowing violet tip pointing at the eye slit. 'Surrender, foe!' she shouted.

The Rannalal commander swiped at her with a short sword. Sophie dodged effortlessly, and let fly with the arrow. It pierced the armour of his left shoulder and he fell from his usrog with a snarl. The eight-legged beast reared up and tried to snag Sophie's feathery feet with the claws on its hoofs. But she slid easily aside as she tugged another arrow from her quiver.

As the Rannalal commander took his swipe, the other skymaids and skyboys swooped down from the trees. Arrows flew thick. Rannalal knights raised their shields. Axes were flung upward. One of the knights even managed to let loose a silver net, which Elsie sliced in half with a sharp cutlass. Several Rannalal fell, their armour pierced. A skymaid cried shrilly as a sword slashed her leg. More arrows rained down. Stricken usrogs stampeded. Blood began to stain the ice.

'Enough,' Taggie groaned, hating the awful violence. Nobody saw her, let alone heard.

The Rannalal gathered together in an expert defensive formation, the outer ring holding their shields out while five archers in the centre took aim at the skyfolk above.

Taggie couldn't take it any more. People were being hurt because of her. She had to do something, even though she hadn't got a clue what that would be. Without thinking, she jumped up on to the rocks above the waterfall. 'Enough!' she roared. 'I am the Queen-to-be, the heir of Usrith. And I say *no more*.'

Rannalal and skyfolk alike paused in the middle of their battle, staring at her. Taggie looked back, equally uncertain. Then two arrows came slicing out of the Rannalal formation. They were aimed true, flying swiftly – which did the archers no good at all.

The arrows reached the enchantment shield Taggie had spun around herself, and burst into flaming ruin. She glared down at the little four-legged knights in their armour. 'I warned you,' she said furiously. Memories rushed into her head, carrying her along. Her hand shot out, finger pointing. '*Ki-Dionak!*'

The ice covering the pond let out an enormous *crack*. It shattered into a thousand pieces, and the Rannalal knights along with their frightened usrogs fell into water as cold as the Arctic. Heavy red armour dragged the Rannalal down. They thrashed about frantically, barely managing to keep their heads above the bobbing fragments of ice.

Taggie gasped at what she'd done. Then she began to worry that one of the little knights would drown. '*Ti-Hath.*' She commanded hurriedly, and the pond surface immediately refroze, locking the Rannalal knights into place.

Jemima lifted her head cautiously over the rocks and pushed her lips together as she took in the imprisoned knights. 'Wow, Taggie, you really *are* getting good at this,' she said approvingly.

16

THE REFUGEE CAMP

The camp was deep inside the Farndorn Forest; so deep, Taggie was amazed they'd even managed to find it. The refugees from the town of Charavik had built themselves dome-like shacks from branches and mud, which were now covered in a thin layer of snow, providing natural camouflage. You could be walking between them before you realized you were in the middle of a rebel village.

Soon after the young skyfolk had chopped the Rannalal knights out of the ice one by one, they'd met up with a troop of Dolvoki Rangers who were helping to guard the forest. The rangers were only too happy to help escort the prisoners. Jemima had been intrigued by the rangers, who were tall and slim, with long pointed ears and shining green eyes with cat-like irises. Mr Anatole led the way into the camp, sturdy and resolute at the head of the procession. Taggie and Jemima followed with a pair of Dolvoki Rangers walking beside them, and Sophie with her cousins flying overhead.

The sisters were still wearing their high-vis quilted Outer Realm coats, which made them stand out. People came hurrying out of their shacks to stare. A great flock of adult skyfolk came swooping down from their nests in the trees overhead, greeting their children. Taggie saw Sophie's father embrace her with a fearsomely strong grip. He was a slight man, just like all the skyfolk, his arms and legs beginning to turn opaque with age. His bald head was covered in intricate silver tattoos. When he landed, the feathers of his broad fin-like feet folded up neatly, so that they looked almost like human ones.

'You were just supposed to patrol the edge of the wood and raise the alarm should anyone come,' he chided his daughter. 'Not attack Rannalal knights. Don't ever *ever* do anything so foolhardy again.'

'Yes, Dad,' Sophie agreed meekly. At which he hugged her even tighter.

Sophie rolled her eyes and pulled a face for Taggie; a face which said: *See what I have to put up with!*

Taggie smiled back shyly. The sight made her miss her own dad even more. She walked apprehensively towards what looked like the main shack, along a path lined by hundreds of different kinds of people who were all jostling together good-naturedly. She wished she could give them reassuring regal smiles, which was no doubt what they were expecting, rather than the hesitant grin which was all she seemed able to manage.

The first man she tentatively shook hands with was almost as furry as a bear, and she became embarrassed by his gratitude. He was next to a family whose tails flicked about nervously. Then there were some people who were completely round, with heads that barely had a neck. A group of giants were eager to greet her, hooting and waving above the heads of everyone else, and she held her hand out nervously, but they were very gentle. Surprisingly, there were even a few Rannalal women with their children, so she made sure she said hello to them too – though it was hard. All along the path, children stared and pointed in awe as their parents whispered to them.

'Say something,' Jemima muttered out of the side of her mouth.

'Like what?' Taggie hissed back. It was all she could do to keep walking. The idea of running back into the forest was extremely appealing.

'*Hello* would be a start.'

Taggie looked round at the hopeful eager faces. She gulped, knowing she had to say something. 'Hello. I'm Taggie, Prince Dino's daughter, and this is my younger sister Jemima.'

The cheer that went up was a loud and joyful one indeed. It was as if a dam had broken. Everyone applauded enthusiastically. People rushed forward to greet the sisters, hugging them, kissing them, telling them how happy they were to see them, how honoured that they'd come to this forest camp. Many were crying openly. Most had words of thanks for standing up to the terrible King of Night and his followers. Everyone pledged their allegiance to the one true Queen-to-be.

It took a long time to reach the main shack in the middle of the camp.

Jemima watched Taggie being led inside by Wenuthi Jones, the chief of the Dolvoki Rangers, and several other important people from the camp. The welcome they'd been given was generous, but she was very aware of how most of it had been directed at Taggie, not her. Oh, everyone was pleased to see her, but it was really Taggie they were in awe of, their Queen-to-be.

She was just about to follow when something made her turn aside from the shack – after all, it wasn't as if anyone in there would miss her. She walked through the camp, looking at all the people milling round. Sure enough, nobody came searching to see where she'd gone – not even Felix. After a minute she came to a shack that seemed no different to any other. Cautiously she pushed aside the curtain that covered the entrance and peered inside.

A small fire burned in the centre of the earth floor, wisps of smoke curling up to vanish through clever slits at the apex. On the other side of the flames was an old woman wrapped in a dark cloak over a purple velvet dress. Her raven hair was flecked with grey strands, and the skin on her face was as thick and dark as leather. Both ears were completely covered in gold studs and pierced by hoops. More hoops went through her nose. Jemima couldn't help grinning: she looked like a punk rocker's grandma.

'Hello,' Jemima said. 'Who are you?'

'You tell me,' the woman said flatly.

'What?'

'Tell me who I am.'

Jemima's good humour began to fade. 'I don't know.'

'Yes you do, Blossom Princess. Tell me. Now!'

'Mrs Veroomes,' Jemima said quickly. She frowned, unsure how that name had come out of her mouth.

All the sternness seemed to leave Mrs Veroomes, and she smiled the way any teacher would when a difficult pupil got something right. 'Quite right, my dear, that's me. I've been waiting here for you this whole last week. And I was many days on the road from Lorothain to get here. Not a pleasant journey, I assure you, not in these times; not even for someone like me. I had to spend half my time hopping smartly behind hedges or into ditches, waiting for the Rannalal patrols, or worse, to pass. But it was worth it, I saw you'd come here to this camp eventually.'

'What do you mean, someone like you?'

Mrs Veroomes gave Jemima a long chiding stare, silent and expectant.

'Oh,' Jemima mumbled. 'You're a seer.'

'Yes, my dear.'

'But how did you find us? Taggie said she enchanted us against seers.'

'Ha!' Mrs Veroomes dismissed the notion with a wave of her hand. 'All due respect to your esteemed sister, but this is not her art. It is yours and mine. Now come in and sit with me, my dear. We have a lot to talk about, and I've made tea and toast. It doesn't take a seer to know you're hungry.'

Jemima sat on some cushions while the old woman lifted an iron kettle off the fire. 'My dad said in his letter that I should come and see you,' she said.

'Ah yes, the Prince Dino. How nice he remembered me, for I remember him very well indeed,' Mrs Veroomes said as she rescued some thick slices of bread that were impaled on a toasting fork over the flames. She started scraping off the burnt edges.

'You do?' Jemima said, suddenly intrigued. 'Tell me, please.'

'Many years ago he came to me, not long after I started helping my mother. A very determined boy, he was. He said he'd met the most amazing girl who'd saved his life, and that he had to seek her out again to say thank you if nothing else. He was cross that his mother had forbidden him to do so. Like all impetuous boys, the more something is not allowed, the more he wanted it. He'd tried using some runes an aunt had given him, but he never had the sight, not like you or I. So by the time he came to me he was quite desperate.'

'He meant Taggie!' Jemima exclaimed. 'We were there yesterday, fighting Rannalal knights at the palace. The

Great Gateway, Arasath, sent us into the past.'

'Ah,' Mrs Veroomes said, handing over the toast. 'I did wonder what deeper magic was at play. I could never find the girl for him, even though I spent many weeks trying to sight her. I thought, back then, that I lacked my mother's art. It was most discouraging. And your father was by turns angry and dejected by my failure.'

'I'm not surprised you couldn't find us,' Jemima said around the toast she was chewing on. 'We weren't even born then.'

Mrs Veroomes passed over a delicate china cup of green tea. 'However, I was fated to catch but one brief glimpse of the girl in a strange place I took to be the Outer Realm. It was a strong sight, mind, restoring my faith in myself and my art. So then I could face the prince with dignity that final time he came to me, and provide the answer he craved.'

'That's when he left the First Realm, isn't it?'

Mrs Veroomes nodded silently. 'Nobody knew where he'd gone. His mother, the Queen, was frantic, believing him to have been taken by some dark force. She consulted many seers, who never glimpsed him; it is very difficult to see into the Outer Realm, for it is not a place that welcomes magic. Her Holvan guards were sent far and wide across many realms to try and find him; they were so anxious. They didn't, of course.'

'Didn't Grandma ask you?' Jemima asked, enthralled by the story.

'I was only a girl back then. And of course the longer I left it without telling anyone, the more difficult it would be to explain my part in his disappearance. I always thought he'd come right back. But he never did. I caught the occasional glimpse of him down the years – always sad, always looking for the girl – so I knew he was alive, and that there was a true heir to the shell throne. I believed everything would come good in the end and he would come home to take his rightful place upon the shell throne.' She gave Jemima an ashamed glance. 'How wrong I was. What a useless seer I turned out to be.'

'No,' Jemima said, concerned by the woman's misery. 'Not for me. If Daddy hadn't gone to the First Realm he wouldn't have met my mum.' She smiled encouragingly. 'I wouldn't be here.'

Mrs Veroomes drank her tea in silence for a moment. 'That's true,' she said finally. 'And what a blessing you are, Blossom Princess.'

'Do you think I'm a seer, too?' Jemima asked.

'I don't speculate about you at all, my dear. You saw your way to me. You tell me what that makes you.'

The ranger chief's large shack had several benches around its central fire. Birds and rabbits were roasting on spits above the flames. As soon as she saw them, Taggie realized just how hungry she was.

The ranger chief, Wenuthi Jones, gave her a plate of bread and slices of hot meat, which she tucked into heartily. Mr Anatole was also enjoying his meal. As Taggie ate she realized everyone was watching her, and became conscious of how fast she was eating.

'Thank you very much,' she said when she'd finished.

'My Queen-to-be . . .' The ranger chief bowed as he recovered the plate. Taggie smiled at the man; he had the weathered face of someone who spent a lot of time outdoors. She was sure she could see the top of a scar just above the collar of his shirt, but didn't want to stare for fear of being rude.

'So what now?' she asked.

'Majesty, I have already sent word to other refugee encampments,' Wenuthi Jones said. 'Soon the news of your arrival will be heard by all the peoples of the First Realm. The Karrak Lords and Ladies will fear the rejoicing which will ring out. It will only be a matter of time until the Kings and Queens of the other Realms pledge you their armies.'

'Armies?' Taggie gave Mr Anatole a desperate glance. The old equerry cleared his throat and gave the assembled dignitaries a troubled look. 'Our Queen-to-be wishes it to be known most firmly she does not countenance war. She is destined to become a Queen of Dreams, not of anguish.'

'But Majesty, your people are in anguish now under the so-called King of Night's regime,' said Piadrow, Sophie's father. 'Every day more of the dark hordes arrive from the Fourth Realm and claim the homes and lands of your people.'

'I'm really sorry, I don't know the history of the Realms,' Taggie told him. 'What's the Fourth Realm?'

'A pleasant and prosperous land once upon a time,' Felix said softly. Taggie saw the others in the shack give the white squirrel embarrassed glances before they politely turned their heads away.

'What happened?' she asked him gently.

'It fell to darkness generations ago,' Felix said. 'Now the sky is iron grey and ice grips the land. The Karraks and their followers banished spring and summer on the day of their victory against our noble houses, and winter has reigned ever since. Winter and evil. The Fourth Realm has become the nest of all darkness in these fine realms. Always the Karrak Lords and their minions seek the cracks in decency so they can worm their way out into other realms, exploiting weaknesses and corrupting the faint-hearted. It is a great sadness we didn't know of your existence until now, Princess. If we had, the reign of the Queens of Dreams would not have been broken and challenged by Lord Jothran.'

'So you're saying more and more dark creatures will come here as long as Jothran sits upon the throne?' Taggie asked.

'Majesty,' Mr Anatole said in his gurgling voice. 'That is where our greatest hope lies. Jothran has not yet sat upon the shell throne of the First Realm. He cannot do so, for while your bloodline remains intact the throne remains closed to him.'

'You mean while Jem and I are alive?'

'Yes, Majesty. That is why he took your father. There

is a certain ceremony, a dark depraved ceremony, that he will perform to prise the throne open, thus obtaining complete control over the deep magic which governs this realm. Once he has that power, he will truly be able to claim his title of King of Night.'

Taggie closed her eyes. 'I think I can feel the moonclouds,' she said faintly. 'But they seem wrong, somehow, not as my ancestors' memories have them.'

'The wizardry of the Karrak Lords and Ladies has bound them together, my Queen-to-be,' Piadrow said. 'It takes a lot of their strength, but they hold them fast.'

'I used to be able to cloudbust in the Outer Realm,' Taggie said. 'I even did it here once, when I visited before. But I don't think I can do it now. I'm sorry. I'm not strong enough.'

'If you were to sit on the throne,' Felix said, 'you would be at one with this Realm's nature and gain that strength.'

'But how could that be? How could I sit upon the shell throne?' Taggie asked, knowing full well what the answer would be.

'An army could storm the palace and return you to your rightful place,' Wenuthi Jones informed her solemnly.

'There has to be another way,' gasped Taggie.

'Majesty, the throne room is the ancient keep at the very heart of the palace,' Mr Anatole said. 'It is the most heavily guarded building in all of the First Realm. I know this for I have lived within the palace for over half of my life. The old walls used to be a fortified castle built just after the First Times. They were subsequently built around and upon, made elegant and pleasing to the eye by later Princes and Queens; but at their core they are still unbreakable walls of thick stone and heavy enchantments. Enchantments which are now reinforced by the wizardry of the Karraks themselves. The ranger chief is correct: it will take an army. A very large army.'

'And how long would it take to gather an army of such a size? Weeks? Months? Years? How long does my father have before Jothran sacrifices him?'

'The King of Night now knows that it is pointless to kill your father, Princess,' Felix said with his tail tip twitching. 'Your father's blood alone will not open the throne. It is you he fears now.'

'I came here to get my father *back*,' Taggie said. 'After he's safe . . . then I will listen to your arguments in favour of war.'

'That is a worthy notion, Majesty,' Wenuthi Jones said. 'And I admire your nobility and determination. But we cannot rescue your father.'

'Why not?'

'Put simply . . . we don't know where he is. The Karrak Ladies cast deceitful enchantments which prevent our strongest seers from foretelling his whereabouts.'

At that moment the thick curtain over the shack's entrance was pushed aside. Jemima came in, followed by Mrs Veroomes.

'I know where Daddy is!' she said.

17

A DREAMING PRINCESS

Taggie didn't know if she should laugh or cry at Jemima's claim. In the end she just settled for a weary, 'Where?'

'In the palace,' Jemima said excitedly.

'Nobody doubts you, Blossom Princess,' Mr Anatole said. 'But it is a big palace.'

'I can find him,' Jemima said. She held up the suede purse. 'I've got my runes.'

'Oh, Jem . . .' Taggie began in dismay.

'I can! Mrs Veroomes has shown me how to read runes. Well . . . some of them. And I promised Grandma I would practise until I understood the art. You were there.'

Taggie gave Wenuthi Jones a pleading look.

'Sweet Blossom Princess,' the ranger chief said kindly. 'Those with a lifetime of experience cannot see into the darkness of the palace. Even Mrs Veroomes here, whose accomplishments are legendary, could find nothing.'

'Quite true,' Mrs Veroomes said. 'I cannot. However, I am not of the prince's family. A family bond will always shine through the darkness; nothing is stronger than that.'

'He's in the dungeons,' Jemima said. 'Really he is. I saw him. He's all dirty and tired, and sitting in this horrid stone room all by himself. But he's alive. Isn't that the most wonderful thing?'

The feeling of relief somehow took all the strength out of Taggie's limbs. But she managed to smile foolishly.

'Even if you are right, Blossom Princess,' Mr Anatole said, 'there are many, many cells, vaults and dungeons beneath the palace. Even I am not familiar with the maze of passages down there. To search them all could take weeks. You would have minutes at most, that's if you ever got inside. The palace is guarded by regiments of the Karrak Lords' followers. Nothing can enter or leave unchallenged.'

Jemima's sandy hair flopped down over her face. She looked at Taggie with desperation in her tired eyes. 'We have to rescue Daddy. If I'm there I can guide you to the right dungeon, I swear I can.'

Taggie turned to Piadrow. 'Could you fly us in?'

'I could, Majesty. Skyfolk would be able to land in the castle courtyards or on the towers, and many flocks would come with you . . . but not unseen. The alarm would be given, and we would have to fight our way to the dungeons.'

Taggie nearly said, 'Then what do we do?' in a whiney voice but something made her hold her tongue. Princess Elizabeth would never act all needy and desperate; she wouldn't plead. And Mr Koimosi always told her to use her opponents' strength against them. Not that everyone gathered in the shack were enemies – far from it – but they were opposing her. They were all soldiers and advisers with lifetimes of experience.

Taggie gathered her thoughts and gave Wenuthi Jones a level gaze. 'How would you suggest we get into the dungeons without raising suspicion?'

The discussion of how to sneak into the palace went on for hours. Wenuthi Jones, Piadrow and Felix argued and planned, with Taggie and Mr Anatole making suggestions. Eventually preparations were set in motion.

Wenuthi Jones insisted it be kept simple; that way there was less to go wrong, he explained. They would capture a party of Ethanu and wear their clothes, assuming their identity. Then they would ride right into the palace with a ranger as their 'prisoner' and go straight to the dungeons. Once they found Prince Dino, Piadrow and the hardiest of his flock would fly down into the courtyard and whisk them all safely away.

'To get in unchallenged is one thing,' Piadrow said solemnly. 'To get out is another entirely.'

Everyone was content about that part of the plan, giving it their wholehearted approval – just as they were unanimously horrified when Taggie and Jemima insisted on being part of the break-in party. But Jemima was the only one who could sight her father's exact location, and Taggie wasn't going to let her go alone.

Eventually Mr Anatole saw how tired the sisters were, and everyone else was ushered out of the shack. Taggie and Jemima were shown to a curtained-off area where cots had been prepared for them. They just managed to get their boots off before collapsing on to the soft furs.

And so for the first time in her life, Taggie Paganuzzi fell asleep in the First Realm. She was expecting all her worry and anxiety over her father and the Karrak Lords (Golzoth especially) to trouble her dreams. Instead, she witnessed the dreams of others as their nightmares poured disquiet and fears out into the merciless night. Her little heart went out to them in sympathy, and deep in sleep she told them not to worry, promising she would do what she could to ease their suffering.

Those closest in the Farndorn rebel camp came to her first. Taggie found herself in a peaceful forest glade, with a warm sun streaming through the overhead beech leaves to dapple the grass, while flutterseeds drifted idly through the air, getting in the way of bees laden with pollen. A little boy, no more than four years old, was lying in the middle of the glade, curled up asleep, and crying.

Taggie woke him, and he clung to her. 'What's the matter?' she asked, and carefully wiped his tears away with her hand.

'It's always cold and dark now,' he said, 'And my dad's away in the trees fighting the dark enemy. I'm frightened. He might not come back.'

Taggie hugged him close. 'Sweetheart, did you know I'm going to be the next Queen of Dreams? I'm going to sit on the shell throne, and bring the sun back. When I do,

the snow will melt, and your dad will return. Then you can go home again.'

The child gazed up at her in delight. 'Really? You're the Queen-to-be? I saw you arrive in the camp today, my mother said who you are, but I wasn't sure if you really were.'

'I am.'

'And you care about me?'

'I care about everybody.'

He gave her an adoring gaze. Taggie stroked him gently, soothing him back to sleep. When he closed his eyes he was smiling, and breathing easily. There were no more tears.

She got up and turned to see one of the giant men with green hair. He was kneeling down, his big head bowed, shoulders shaking.

'What's the matter?' she asked compassionately.

'My Queen, I have seen terrible things.'

Taggie hugged him, even though he was so broad her arm barely covered half his back. 'Why don't you tell me about it?' she said. 'If I can help, I will.'

So it went. Every sleeping child that whimpered in fright at the cruelty of their new rulers she lulled with the gentle conviction that ultimately the King of Night would not ruin their lovely realm. To every mother clutching her babe in fear of the future, she whispered reassuringly that light would soon dawn to replace darkness. Finally, to the men who raged silently at their own helplessness, she gave assurance that the time would soon come to reclaim everything that had been torn savagely from their grasp.

Only then, only after the First Realm had witnessed their new Queen-to-be, and taken comfort from her generous compassion as was their privilege, did Taggie Paganuzzi finally sink into a tranquil slumber.

She awoke feeling amazingly refreshed. That surprised her, for she remembered sharing her dream with a multitude, and expected such an effort would be exhausting. Instead it was immensely satisfying, knowing she had helped so many people face a new day with renewed optimism and courage.

When she emerged from her cot, everyone stopped to look at her and bowed respectfully. It was hugely embarrassing.

Jemima broke the silence. 'I never really understood what our grandmother did before,' she said. 'But you were fabulous, Taggie. I wish the Outer Realm had someone like you. There wouldn't be all those wars then.'

'My Queen,' Wenuthi Jones said in reverential greeting. 'We have breakfast prepared for you.'

'Thank you.'

The tough ranger blushed. 'Last night, when I dreamed of telling you about my son . . .'

Taggie couldn't remember any of the individual encounters, just like ordinary dreams they remained unobtainable during the day. 'Did I help?' she asked cautiously.

'Oh yes,' he said sincerely. 'To me you are not a Queen-to-be. You are already our Queen of Dreams.'

Taggie looked at the hard earth floor, too self-conscious to meet the ranger's eyes. Yet, at the same time she felt so *good* for what she'd done.

'Try the nutflakes,' Jemima said. 'They're like the best muesli ever. And the scrambled eggs are so creamy.'

'Thank you,' Taggie said as she sat at one of the benches.

Sophie brought a bowl over and gave her a dainty bow.

'Don't go,' Taggie said quickly. 'Please, sit with us.' She desperately needed someone with a sense of humour amid so many serious adults.

'Love to.' Sophie grinned, and sat down on the bench beside Taggie. Her big wings flapped very slowly, showing off their iridescent sheen; somehow they always managed to avoid the strands of her hair that were constantly waving about as if she was in the middle of her own breeze. 'You know Dad spent half the night organizing our folk to fly to other encampments and spread the word of your arrival. None of them needed to go as everyone knows you are here now.'

'Tell him I'm sorry.'

'No need. I haven't seen him this happy for ages. Just knowing a new Queen of Dreams exists is such a blessing to this realm. Thank you for coming.'

Taggie shrugged and tucked into her nutflakes.

'There are a lot of people outside wanting to meet you,' Sophie continued. 'Artisans mostly. They've all got gifts for you.'

Jemima perked up at that. 'Gifts?'

'They shouldn't have,' Taggie said round a mouthful of the cereal, and giving her sister a stern glance. 'They have so little for themselves out here in the forest.'

'Don't be too quick to turn them down,' Sophie said with a twinkle in her eyes. 'Some of them could be very useful. Talveral the smith has some amazing armour for Jemima.'

Taggie immediately thought of the Rannalal knights and shuddered. 'I suppose I should meet some of them,' she agreed.

'But I don't want armour!' Jemima protested.

'Talveral's gift is the greatest you will ever be given,' Sophie said. 'The armour is woven from *athrodene*, which is the heart of an angel. This is the same armour the Irradok princess-captains wore when they sailed to battle with the Paxia during the war of the Vewass Archipelago.' She grinned wistfully as her long red hair continued to wave gracefully around her head. 'Now that was a time I would have liked to see.'

'Where is the Vewass Archipelago?' Taggie asked. She was beginning to feel like an oaf by not knowing the history of the Realms. When this was over she knew she'd have to lock herself away for a year just to read the history books.

'In the Realm of Air,' Sophie said longingly. 'That's where the angels first brought the skyfolk, it's our natural home.' She wrinkled her nose up, which pushed a lot of cute freckles close together. 'One day I'll visit.'

'Don't you like it here?'

'Oh yes, the First Realm is so beautiful . . .' She paused. 'That is, it used to be. And it will be again now you're here. I'll fight with you to make it right again.'

'Do you think I'm weak for wanting to avoid war?' Taggie asked.

Sophie leaned in closer, her hair swirling as it followed the motion like an airborne cloak. 'I think that makes you the strongest out of everyone in the camp. But I just don't see how you can do it without war. Sorry. But then I've never seen magic as strong as yours back at the frozen pool. I expect you could even blast a Karrak Lord to cinders. Hey! Do you suppose that's the way to do it? You could duel against Jothran.'

'Majesty!' Mr Anatole said from behind them, giving Sophie a furious look. 'That is not a course of action you should be considering.'

Both girls gave a guilty start. Taggie hadn't seen the old equerry come over to their table. 'No,' she said slowly as she thought about it. 'No, actually it's not.'

'No?' Sophie asked, sounding disappointed.

'No. Whatever we do, however we seek to overthrow the Karrak Lords, it has to be a method that guarantees success, and I have no idea if I can defeat Jothran. All those people I dreamed for last night . . . I promised them so much. I can't keep those promises if I'm dead.'

A long sigh of relief escaped from Mr Anatole's throat. 'Majesty. I am pleased you begin to understand what your position entails. Now if you would—'

'No,' Taggie said quickly. 'I am not reconsidering rescuing my father. And I will be leading the break-in party.'

'Yes, Majesty.'

After breakfast they went outside. The Dolvoki Rangers were getting their horses ready for the trek to Lorothain.

'Over a thousand men volunteered to join us, Majesty,' Wenuthi Jones said. 'Everyone in this camp, in fact. They will do anything to help you.'

'A thousand people?' Taggie said, startled by the number. 'This is supposed to be a secret mission.'

'I know. That's why it will just be a chosen few of my

rangers escorting you to the outskirts of Lorothain; that way we can ride swiftly and without attracting attention. Meanwhile, the main troop of volunteers will be part of a grand procession travelling to the Estwial Sea, making it look like you're going to visit the port cities to raise support and more troops.'

Elsie the skymaid fluttered overhead, grinning broadly. 'I've volunteered to be you,' she said. 'I'm going to dress up in the fanciest dress we can find, and ride on a big white horse at the front of the procession. There will be knights and squires clustering round, just like they would a real Queen.'

Wenuthi Jones smiled stoically. 'Hopefully, Jothran will send his forces out after them, leaving us free to carry out our mission quietly and without attention.'

'I will lead some of my flock to fly above you,' Piadrow assured her. 'We'll be able to spot any of the enemy's forces approaching; that way you can take cover and avoid any conflict.'

'We have been getting troubling reports all morning,' Wenuthi Jones said. 'It would seem your arrival in the First Realm has angered the King of Night. His patrols have turned savage, they are laying waste to towns and farms alike, buildings have been burned for no reason and many hostages taken, with children torn from their parents.'

'Oh no,' Taggie said. 'That's awful, and it's all my fault. I shouldn't have dreamed last night.' The prospect was so painful, everything she'd done in her dream had been so natural, and felt so right. She had helped people when they needed it most, when they were alone and vulnerable, which was what she truly wanted.

'No, Majesty,' Mr Anatole said swiftly in his gurgling voice. 'The King of Night would have known you were here anyway. You are the Queen-to-be. You are the truth of this precious Realm. It is time the Karrak usurper understood that. Already he must realize his followers cannot enslave everyone: the more misery and suffering he unleashes, the more your peoples' resolve against him hardens.'

'I suppose so,' Taggie said, though she wasn't convinced.

One of the first gifts she received was a saddle for the journey. Suede riding trousers, softer than silk, were another offering. Both she and Jemima finally got rid of their gaudy Outer Realm coats, replaced by long leather coats that Taggie considered disturbingly similar to those worn by the Ethanu. But at least they wouldn't be so visible against the grey ice and snow. And they had hoods lined by thick fluffy wool that kept the freezing air off their heads.

Jemima swiftly changed her mind about armour when she finally saw the suit of *athrodene*. Felix had led her across the camp to the tall tepee which housed Talveral the smith. She didn't quite have the confidence to simply find her way with only her seer ability guiding her. But Felix was happy enough to lead her, and unlike Taggie, he never teased her.

'How come you already know your way around the

camp?' she asked him. 'Don't squirrels sleep?'

He turned and regarded her with those unnervingly black eyes set deep in his white fur. 'Just as much as you do,' he replied. 'But every good agent needs to be familiar with the area he's in. I took a quick scout round last night.'

'Have you been on many missions before this one?'

'No. I was still in my training year when the darkness started to emerge. I did escort some of your distant cousins to the palace in the hope the shell throne would open for them. Alas it did not.'

'Why not?'

'Because it knew your grandmother's direct bloodline was intact. Actually, that it did not open brought hope to those of us loyalists remaining. We set out one last time to search for your father. All of us swore we would not return unless we were triumphant. I little thought it would be me who succeeded, though this is a bitter victory.'

'How long were you looking?'

Felix twitched his whiskers. 'Three and a half years.'

'Gosh.' Jemima didn't really know what else to say. 'I'm glad it was you who found us.'

'This is Talveral's tent,' Felix announced, and pulled back the entrance flap to the tepee.

Jemima went in. It was hot inside and full of acrid smoke coming from the glowing coals heating a central forge. 'You might have warned me,' she said, unbuttoning her coat. She turned round and saw a teenage boy with long white flowing hair holding the tepee flap open behind her. He was dressed in a simple tunic of suede the colour of pine bark, with thin moccasins on his feet.

'Oh,' she said. 'Are you the apprentice?'

'Blossom Princess!' a booming voice said.

Jemima looked round to see Talveral approaching across the tepee; he was a big man with a ruddy sweating face, hands calloused from wielding the heavy tools of his trade. 'I am Talveral, and I welcome you to my home. Hopefully just a temporary home now you and the Queen-to-be have come.'

Jemima frowned awkwardly. It was very disturbing to have everyone she met expecting them to bring salvation. She didn't think she'd ever get used to that. 'Thank you.'

She turned back to the apprentice. But the boy had vanished. Felix stood inside the closed tepee flap. His white fur had fluffed out all over from the heat.

'It is such an honour,' Talveral said. 'As soon as I heard you were here I knew I had to give you the armour. It is perfect for you.'

'Er, thank you . . .' Jemima checked round the inside of the tepee, but the white-haired apprentice boy was nowhere to be seen.

'This way, Blossom Princess.' Talveral gestured with a half-bow, his open, generous face smiling expectantly.

The *athrodene* suit was actually a chain-mail vest and trousers. Talveral told her it was made from a piece of an angel's heart which his great-grandfather claimed to have brought back from the Realm of Air. It had taken decades to craft, he said. First enchanting the piece so that flakes would fall free, then forging each flake into a ring amid flames from the hottest burning coals combined with a secret blend of herbs his family had passed down between them for generations. Indeed, it had been Talveral's father who started making the armour.

When Jemima saw the vest and trousers hanging over the side of a chest she could've sworn they were a translucent silver, but then when she put them on they'd somehow become a grubby white. She held an arm up, frowning at it. 'But . . .'

'It blends into the colour of the wearer's background, Princess,' Talveral explained proudly. 'Which makes it very hard to see. And unlike a shadecasting, cannot be counter-charmed.'

'Thank you,' Jemima said happily. 'It's fabulous. And so light, too.'

'You and your sister are the hope of our Realm,' Talveral said with a grin. 'I cannot allow you to be harmed.'

A minute later Jemima was running across the camp.

'Look at this,' she exclaimed to Taggie who was saddling up her horse.

'It's very *you*,' Taggie said to her sister, who now looked slightly comical in snow-coloured chain mail made for someone a lot taller and wider.

'Don't snark,' Jemima said, and picked up a big stick. She whacked it across her legs. The *athrodene* mail instantly hardened all over, and the stick rebounded.

Taggie pursed her lips in admiration. 'Wow,' she admitted. 'That is quite impressive.' It was also a huge relief: she'd been worried about taking Jemima along, unsure if her own shield invocations could be spun out to include her sister. Now at least she could be confident about any stray arrows and axes.

'Told you,' Sophie said with a wink as she hovered just above them, her wings a haze, they beat so rapidly. The skymaid was in a very cheery mood. It had taken an hour of pleading, but her father had finally allowed her to accompany them on the trip to Lorothain.

'But no further,' he'd warned. 'You are not helping with the prince's rescue.'

'I understand,' Sophie had sworn faithfully.

Wenuthi Jones had dispatched the decoy troop, who would emerge from the Farndorn Forest within the hour, making their noisy way towards the coast a hundred and fifty miles away. Taggie and her small escort, meanwhile, would wind their way quietly through the valleys of the vast forest, and come out on the other side of the hills, fifteen miles or so from the capital city.

Taggie and Jemima mounted up with the ten rangers chosen as their escort. They had been given a couple of sweet-tempered chestnut mares to ride. Taggie patted and soothed hers as she'd been taught at the riding school a year ago. Mr Anatole slipped easily on to the saddle of his own horse beside her. Felix scampered up on to a saddle-less pony, and held on to its shaggy mane. Talveral the smith and Wenuthi Jones had to help Mrs Veroomes off the top of a wide tree stump and on to her horse. Taggie thought she looked like a gothic gypsy bride as she sat unsteadily in the saddle.

'Are you all right?' Taggie asked. She wasn't entirely sure the old seer lady should be coming with them, but didn't quite know how to say no. Everyone else seemed quite content to have her along. And Jem was already treating her like a substitute grandmother.

'Quite all right, thank you, Majesty,' Mrs Veroomes replied. 'Besides, you need me a lot more than you do these fine rangers.'

Taggie glanced round at the imposing Dolvoki Rangers who were mounting up behind her. 'I see,' Taggie said in her best royal tone.

'No, you don't,' Mrs Veroomes said with a chuckle. 'But fortunately I do. I will be diverting the sight of the Karrak Ladies. They have been searching this Realm for you from the moment you started dreaming for us last night.'

'Oh . . .' Taggie blushed. And she was sure she could hear Jem sniggering. 'Thank you.'

Fifteen of the skyfolk took to the air, scattering wide to keep watch on the ground below. The little convoy moved off into the snow-covered forest. Despite the formidable challenge ahead, Taggie couldn't help but smile. This was her quest now, and she was determined to see it through to the end, no matter what.

18

FOREST CREATURES

'Do you know exactly what I have to do when I sit on the throne?' Taggie asked Mr Anatole once they were under way. 'You said once I was sitting on it I could control the nature of the First Realm.'

Mr Anatole pulled a sad face. 'From what I understand, Majesty, you don't *do* anything. You will simply know or feel what is to be done. The throne will certainly know you.'

'Like the charmsward?' Taggie asked.

'Indeed.'

'And that's why it won't allow Jothran to become King?'

'The throne was forged by Usrith in the shape of a shell. It opens for those who carry his blood.'

'Is Usrith in the throne, like the mages who forged the Great Gateways?'

'I don't believe so, no. Not every realm has a magical throne. For instance, the throne of the Third Realm exists for the powerful and terrible Sorceress-Queens to maintain strict order among their various ancient houses. Thousands of years ago, after a series of awful wars, the houses agreed to create a single sovereign, and give her absolute authority by combining to forge a throne, thus giving the Sorceress-Queen power over all houses. It was the only way to end the bitter rivalry between the sorceresses. At the time, the feuding and wars they devoted so much effort to were slowly destroying them, and they finally acknowledged that. Today, each house takes it in turn to seat a sorceress on the throne, thus ending the rivalry. While the Giant King of the Ninth Realm keeps the peace among his barons mainly by controlling their money, so his is a throne of wealth. Now, the elves of the Sixth Realm are interesting in that—'

'Mr Anatole,' Taggie said sternly. She was learning how the old equerry loved his lectures.

'Yes, Majesty?'

'Usrith's throne?'

'Ah, yes, of course. When angels brought people to the First Realm it was a wild, untamed existence. The moonclouds twirled and frothed chaotically, dancing around the sun to no rhythm but their own. There were no seasons. No order. One day it could be as hot as high summer, while the next could bring snow or hurricanes. Nobody could farm properly, or even rely on day and night being regular. Usrith forged the shell throne to tame the moonclouds for the benefit of all. It was a monumental task, even for a mage of his power, and by the time he finished he was old and tired. He stood aside so his daughter, Lucithe, could be the first Queen. A fey and lovely girl, and according to legend a wondrous healer.

Some claimed she was an animal talker, or perhaps part-elf, while others say it was her natural kindness which gave her so much joy from life. Watching her father strive so hard and selflessly bestowed her with great compassion, which the shell throne enriched. When she was Queen she devoted herself to nurturing the sick and injured of all the First Realm's people without prejudice. Her daughter carried on the tradition. Now the ability has become part of your bloodline, Majesty. While princes can always sit on the throne and calm the moonclouds, only Queens can ease our dreams.'

'So my father can actually sit on the throne?'

'Yes – though the situation is a difficult one. The people of the First Realm are accustomed to Queens. Your grandmother was the eighth Queen in succession, the longest unbroken line in our history. Before that there were short gaps where princes ruled while their daughters grew to age. But everyone knew there was a Queen-to-be, and was content with that. With Prince Dino missing, and the succession unknown, it has been a troubled time since your grandmother passed away.'

Taggie stared up through the frosty branches at the bruised grey sky above the forest. 'Which Jothran and the other Karrak Lords took advantage of?'

'Yes, Majesty, I'm afraid so. Without anyone sitting on the shell throne, the rhythms of the moonclouds, which had been established over generations, became fragile. You have already felt the power of Karrak wizardry. The

Karraks use their powers to distort the gentle hold your family once exerted upon the moonclouds; yet these moonclouds twist and churn as they strive to return to their natural state. All Jothran can do is hold them fast, and squeeze them together, which aids him greatly. But what he desires most is for the throne to open to him, and its full power to be his alone. If he succeeds, this Realm will be swallowed by permanent darkness. To sleep will be to know fear.'

'But the shell throne remains closed against him?' Taggie said.

'Yes. It knows the heirs of Usrith are still alive, for it is bound to you no matter where you live. If he is to open the shell and sit upon it, that blood bond must be broken.'

Taggie gave Jemima a guilty glance, seeing her sister chatting away to the Dolvoki Ranger unlucky enough to be riding beside her. The poor man looked very bemused. 'So if I die, Jem could sit on the throne?'

'Yes, my lady.'

'So there is still hope.'

'Majesty,' Mr Anatole said with great difficulty. 'The risk from both of you venturing into the palace to rescue your father . . .'

'I know,' Taggie said in a tiny voice.

Piadrow flew down through the branches to hover beside Taggie. 'Majesty, my folk report a band of elves are gathering in the forest some way ahead. They seem to know you are close by and have asked us if they can meet you.'

'What do we do about them?' Taggie asked, intrigued. She recalled countless stories and films featuring elves – they were all noble woodland folk who sang and made merry, but could also be fearsome warriors.

Mr Anatole and Wenuthi Jones exchanged a troubled look.

'There is no doubt they would make excellent allies,' Wenuthi Jones said slowly. 'If they were interested.'

'Ah, they don't concern themselves with the problems of mortals,' Taggie said. This time she caught the glance they exchanged.

'Not often, Majesty, no,' Wenuthi Jones said. 'They have their own . . . problems.'

Taggie knew she was missing something. 'Felix, should we meet them?'

Felix joined in the exchange of awkward looks with Wenuthi Jones and Mr Anatole; his tail flopped from one side of his pony to the other. 'I don't see any reason to do so, ma'am,' he said cautiously. 'But then, equally, there's no reason not to. They won't betray us to the Karraks, if that's what you're worried about.'

Taggie turned to Piadrow. 'You say they want to meet me?'

'Yes, Majesty.'

'Very well. If it won't delay us for too long.' Taggie spurred her horse on, excitement rising in her blood. Elves! The most elegant and the wisest of all mythical folk. And she was going to see them.

The music came first. *Just as it should do*, Taggie thought. It was how people always stumbled across elves. They'd be marching through the woodlands on some magical adventure, laughing and dancing on the grass under silver moonlight.

She strained to hear the words. It was difficult. The melody was hard to make out: there were several voices singing, but not quite in harmony – which was odd. *Perhaps mortal ears simply can't appreciate such ethereal beauty?* she thought. But no, the tempo wasn't so good either. And now they drew close the lyrics were growing disturbingly familiar . . .

'Is that "Stairway to Heaven"?' she asked herself. It was one of Dad's favourites from his huge collection of old vinyl albums. He didn't have any CDs, and the concept of digital downloads mystified him.

A guitar was being strummed, which seemed ridiculously out of place in the bleak false winter gripping the forest. She looked across at Mrs Veroomes, who wore an expression that was pure schoolmistress disapproval.

When they reached the clearing where the elves were encamped, an amazing sight greeted them. There were elves everywhere, yet they were almost impossible to see. They blended into the tree trunks so perfectly. And not only the trunks, Taggie realized; the gaps between the trees were also their natural habitat, taking on their texture. Or they took on the texture of the gaps – she wasn't sure. But it brought a delighted smile to her lips. Truly they were magical creatures.

With really tuneless voices. And dressed in weird clothes that were all loops of rainbow-shaded cloth with silver and gold woven through. All the better to cavort about as if they were drunk. Which surely they could not be. Not elves.

Taggie's smile faded somewhat at their oafish behaviour. But she marvelled at their astonishing midnight-black hair. It didn't grow on the side of their heads above their ears (pointed ears, she was relieved to see), but to make up for that, the plume (no other way to describe it) of hair on the top of their head grew back into a thick tail that dangled down to the waist.

A loud wobbly cheer went up when she rode her horse into the clearing.

'Yo, she's here!' a voice shouted out.

Now the elves were clambering to their feet – some of them took several attempts. But once they did stand up, there wasn't one of them under seven feet tall.

'Little Queen, welcome.'

'Oh wow. It *is* her.'

'Hey, it's the blossom one, too. Cool!'

'Er, Taggie . . . ' Jemima whispered. 'Are they really elves?'

'It's good to see you, Queen-to-be.'

'Um . . .' Taggie answered uncertainly.

'Felix Weldowen,' one elf said in a slurred voice. 'Still

not lifted that curse, huh, dude?'

'What does it look like?' Felix said irritably.

'Hello there,' a voice said smoothly at Taggie's side.

She turned, trying not to jump. One of the elves was standing beside her, and even though she was on horseback she still had to look up at his face. His skin was a lustrous dark brown – he was the most handsome person she'd *ever* seen.

'Oh, hello,' Taggie said.

'Earl Maril'bo,' he said with a charming smile as he swept a hand round, gesturing at the other elves. 'And this is my band. You must be our new little Queen-to-be.'

'I am,' she said, smiling back, conveniently ignoring the whole *little* thing.

Sophie came fluttering down next to them, hovering so her head was level with the elf's. 'Maril'bo, hi.'

'Sophs, gimme five. Good to see you, girl.'

They smacked hands.

'This is my friend, Taggie, our new Queen-to-be,' Sophie told him.

'Let me help you down,' Earl Maril'bo said.

Taggie allowed him to lift her off the saddle. When she was on the ground, her head barely came up above his waist.

'Thank you for showing up here to see us, little Queen-to-be,' he said. 'That says a lot about you. I can understand you're kinda busy right now.'

'Oh you know how it is . . . thrones to reclaim, bad

guys to thwart.' Taggie bit her lip, not knowing where a sentence that stupid had come from.

'I feel the need, I really do. Those Karrak dudes are bad to the bone – and that's a lot of bone under those spooky cloaks of theirs.'

'So do you rule the elves of the First Realm?' Taggie asked.

Maril'bo's laugh was a lovely deep rich sound. 'Oh no, little Queen-to-be, I don't rule anything. But I am, like, the top arrow skimmer out of all these slackers.'

'Uh huh.' Taggie gave him a closer look. Two of the colourful cloth hoops crossed his chest like bandoliers, with semi-circular daggers and throwing-firestars in holster pockets. Another strap held a bright silver oval shield across his back, almost as tall as he was. In fact, every elf was carrying a similar shield and weapons. 'What's a skimmer?' she asked.

Maril'bo patted the shield proudly. 'No kidding you, little Queen-to-be: you see, you're looking at the champion surfer out of at least ten Realms.'

'Oh, I've just been surfing at the seaside myself,' Taggie said, hoping he'd approve. 'There were some good waves in Cornwall.'

The whole clearing fell silent for a moment. Then everyone was laughing, even the Dolvoki Rangers. Taggie felt a blush creeping up her cheeks despite the cold air.

'Taggie, elves don't surf on water,' Sophie explained kindly. 'They surf rainbows.'

'True, that,' Maril'bo said. 'I can rip me some serious indigo curves on the edge of a storm.'

'Rainbows?' a startled Taggie asked.

'Oh yeah,' Maril'bo chortled. 'It is, like, the most amazing sensation you can know, with the rain flashing by on one side of you and the hot sky on the other, balancing between the two with the wind in your face. Nothing sweeter.'

'That sounds fantastic,' Jemima cried, and slithered down off her horse. 'How do you do that?'

A grinning Maril'bo pulled what Taggie had assumed was his shield off his back and showed it to the sisters. Now she could see it properly, Taggie realized it was a similar shape to a surfboard. But the silver-mirror surface was strange. She could see the slightly curving image of herself standing looking at it, but she had to squint against the brightness – which was wrong. The sky was gloomy, yet she was seeing herself as if it was a summer's afternoon in the forest. A memory rooted in the charmsward tickled her brain, and she understood the enchantment which caused the board to reflect more light than shone on to it – that was how it stayed afloat on the rainbow.

'That's cool,' Taggie said. 'Can I have a go?'

Earl Maril'bo's handsome face turned sorrowful. 'I would love to jump some light with you, little Queen-to-be,' he said sadly. His big hand gestured up to the sky as flakes of snow began to drift down into the clearing. 'But you have to mix sunlight with rain to bake rainbows. And that's all gone now; the darkness and the cold sucked it away from us. Me and my band here, we were thinking of heading on out to another Realm, one where the sun still shines. We'd kinda given up on the First.' Tears glinted in his big soft eyes. 'All this Realm's beauty had been burned away, or so we thought. Then you arrived, drifting in like a song on the breeze to make us smile again.'

Taggie took hold of his big hand. Her fingers couldn't quite close around his wrist. 'Don't give up on the First Realm. This wretched twilight won't last forever. However long it takes, I will stop Jothran from sitting on the shell throne. I will bring the sunlight and the rain back for you.'

Earl Maril'bo hugged her tight. 'I believe in you, little Queen-to-be. After last night, all of us do.' He grinned round at his band, who smiled encouragement and whooped their approval.

Taggie found herself being lifted back into the saddle.

'We'll stay, little Queen-to-be,' Maril'bo said solemnly. 'When you need us, we'll be there for you. Count on it.

Count on us. Count on me. Peace.' He held up a hand, two long fingers pointing defiantly to the thick churning moonclouds.

Taggie grinned up at his lovely face, captivated by his sincerity. 'Peace.'

19

A NIGHT AT THE INN

It took a day for Taggie and her ranger escort to clear the Farndorn Forest. When they did emerge on to the frozen fields beyond, snow was falling thickly, reducing visibility to a couple of hundred metres. But the greatest seers among the Karrak Ladies were searching for them. For her.

'I can feel their questing,' Mrs Veroomes said as the horses plodded on. The soft snowflakes were sticking to her cloak and building small dunes on the wide brim of her purple hat. 'They know you are close – they feel people's delight at your dreams. They are desperate to capture you.' She took a handful of ash from a suede pouch, and cast it into the slow-moving snow so she could watch the particles drift down. 'Many spies creep across the land, spreading poisoned words and making false promises to those they believe to be weak.'

'What about the diversion?' Wenuthi Jones asked. The ranger wore a tight woollen hat against the cold, and a long cloak fastened round his neck with an old tarnished gold chain. He seemed perfectly at ease riding through the snowy forest, but then Taggie couldn't imagine many things bothering the resolute ranger.

Mrs Veroomes waved a hand through the drifting ash, stirring it. She studied the eddies as they spun amid the snow. 'A great battalion is chasing the volunteers along the road to the sea. Several of the dark Lords accompany them.'

'That's good,' the ranger chief said.

'Do the Karrak Lords not try to conceal themselves?' Mr Anatole asked in puzzlement.

Mrs Veroomes frowned, concentrating. 'No.'

'How strange. They normally cast a shade around their loathsome activities.' He looked worried.

Piadrow and Sophie swooped down out of the snow-clotted sky to hover beside the Dolvoki Ranger. 'It's becoming difficult to scout through this,' the skyman said. 'Two of our party have flown ahead as far as the village of Barrowden, four miles yonder. The fields between here and there are clear of any Karrak minions.'

The prospect of getting off her horse and actually lying down on a bed was all that Taggie cared about now. Her saddle was indeed excellently crafted, and the mare a careful ride, but they'd been riding for hours. She was stiff and sore everywhere – and extra places too. Even Jemima had been quiet for the last part of the afternoon, which was telling.

'I know the village,' Wenuthi Jones said. 'There is an inn there, the Green Duke. The landlord is a good man; we can rest there tonight.'

Taggie wanted to put her arms round the gruff ranger and kiss him.

It still seemed to take forever riding over the fields, avoiding the isolated farm houses. Above them, the moonclouds tightened their grip on the sunlight, thickening and darkening until there was barely any light left on the lands below.

A mile outside Barrowden, they crossed the canal that led to the village station.

Taggie looked down the long straight strip of ice, with its spongy banks of frozen reeds and snow-crusted willows looming overhead. She turned to look the other way, where the canal cut cleanly across the countryside. The snow which fell on the ice was over a foot thick, and hadn't been disturbed. 'Where have all the turtles gone?' she asked plaintively.

'They are in their sheds, hibernating,' Felix told her as his paws gently tugged his pony's mane, guiding it along.

'How can the Karrak Lords do this? Why do they want to ruin other people's lives?'

'It is their nature,' the big white squirrel said. 'As it is our nature to delve into mysteries that should never be examined. There is so much history behind this time, Majesty. You cannot put it all right, you simply have to live the best you can – that is what life is for.'

Taggie nodded meekly. 'I think I'm starting to understand that.'

*

The sight of the abandoned canal had been dismaying enough, but Taggie found the state of the village even more shocking. Many of the cheerful stone cottages had been burned out, their shaggy thatch roofs reduced to piles of ash amid the blackened walls, leaving a skeleton of eaves and rafters sticking up out of the ruins. The ones that remained intact were even worse off, Taggie thought. There were *things* growing on the stone walls – slimy mushrooms with crowns bigger than her head that dripped a dark-green milky mucus on to the ground where it trickled over the crusted snow. Toadstools with stems as long as her arm thrust up out of the wooden window ledges, while thick slippery ribbons of algae clung to the mortar between the stone.

'What is this stuff?' she asked, aghast.

'Frost fungus, Majesty,' Felix said with a shudder of revulsion rippling up the fur on his back. 'It was infecting the capital when I left, and now it is spreading. We believe it originally came from the Dark Universe. There are few buildings left in the Fourth Realm that survive its vile growth.'

As they led their horses through the narrow streets, the blind bulbs of the frost fungus stirred, bending slightly like seaweed caught in a current, yet there was nothing in the air but the gentle drift of snow.

Taggie wondered where everyone had gone. Nobody was outside, which was understandable. But no lights were visible in windows, no smoke curled from chimneys.

'Where are they all?' she asked.

'Some remain here, my Queen-to-be,' Mrs Veroomes said. 'I can see them huddled fearfully in their homes. Most have gone, fled to the countryside and forests. Barrowden is close to the capital, many of the Karrak patrols have passed through, burning and pillaging. Those who remain have stout hearts indeed.'

The frost-fungus growths had only just begun to creep up the walls of the Green Duke. The inn's front door was closed and the windows tightly shuttered. Wenuthi Jones knocked quietly. There was no reply. He knocked again.

'We are closed – there is no ale left,' a muffled voice said from inside.

'Ronuld, it's Wenuthi. I have two young girls with me, they need a bed for a night.'

There was a long pause, then the sound of heavy bolts being drawn back. The door opened and a chubby hand thrust a lantern out. Somewhere in the shadows big round eyes blinked.

'Two girls?' Ronuld exclaimed. 'And a small army of your fellow rangers, which you neglected to mention. Wenuthi Jones, you will be the death of me yet.'

'One night,' the ranger said. 'That is all. And a short one at that.'

The door opened wider, and Ronuld the innkeeper emerged from the dark. He was one of the round people, Taggie saw, his head moving from side to side on a short neck that was almost invisible behind drooping folds of chins and cheeks. His short arms waved excitably. 'The dark patrols are everywhere. They already burned my stables, accusing me of harbouring spies. They would have burned the Green Duke itself if they weren't so fond of my ale – not that they ever pay for it.'

Taggie slipped her coat's hood back, and smiled down at the round man. 'Mr Ronuld, I'm truly sorry to have put you in this position, but we really are very tired, and our seer can foretell a patrol coming from a long way off. We will be gone after a few hours, you have my word on it.'

Ronuld's jaw dropped open. 'Our – our Queen-to-be,' he stammered. He tried to drop to one knee, which his bulk made impossible, so he wound up squatting in the snow.

'Please,' Taggie said, clambering down off her horse.

'Get up, it's cold out here. May we come in?'

'Of course, Majesty, of course.'

The skyfolk fluttered down out of the snow, welcoming the refuge afforded by the inn. Rangers busied themselves caring for their horses, then hurried into the warm parlour to join everyone else. Taggie and Jemima claimed a table near the embers of the fire. Felix, Sophie and Mr Anatole sat with them. Wenuthi Jones sat with Mrs Veroomes on the next table, talking earnestly in quiet voices; they seemed to know each other well. The rest of the rangers spread out around the parlour with the skymen who folded their wings down flat while they were indoors.

Ronuld tipped several fresh dry logs on the embers, kicking up a small flurry of sparks which drifted up the wide stone chimney. Then he waved at his nervous son who came in carrying a tray of food. 'I'm sorry there is so little,' he said bitterly as the boy started handing out plates. 'But the Karrak forces plunder us every time they pass through, and there is no more food coming from the farms. Our stores are almost exhausted.'

'This is more than enough,' Taggie assured him as she chewed on a thick slice of bread, with a portion of hard cheese on top. At least there was hot tea.

'I'm worried about us coming here,' she said quietly to Felix as the round man went over to one of the rangers, offering more tea.

Felix looked up from the bowl of seed he was eating. The snow and frost had melted off his fur, which was now looking badly matted. 'If Wenuthi vouches for Ronuld, we have nothing to fear,' the squirrel replied.

'It's not that. As soon as the innkeeper saw me, he knew who I was. So did everyone in the Farndorn camp. If they do, so will the Rannalal and every spy the dark brethren employ.'

'He knew who you were only when you revealed yourself to him. When we venture into the palace, you will be heavily disguised.'

'I suppose so, and I will practise the wardveil. It's just I'd hate to think I'm the one who's going to ruin this. We have to be successful. We cannot fail.'

'All here understand what is at stake, Princess. And I think if catastrophe lay ahead, Mrs Veroomes would see it.'

'Actually,' Jemima said. 'The one thing seers can never see is their own death. Mrs Veroomes told me. Imagine if you could, if you spent your whole life watching the moment approaching. She said it would drive you mad. And she's right.'

'So we don't know if we're going to succeed,' Taggie said miserably.

'It is a good plan,' Sophie said. 'And the most steadfast of my flock will be waiting above the palace to lift you away from any trouble.'

Taggie smiled at her friend. 'Yes – yes, you're right. I'm sorry . . . I'm just tired and worried.'

'You have every right to be,' Sophie said. 'But we're

here to help in any way we can.'

Taggie looked round the stone-walled parlour, lit only by a few flickering candles and the fire in the hearth. Skyfolk and rangers were starting to relax as they ate their small meal, saying little but united in one cause. She cursed herself for not showing them enough gratitude during the day. They had come with her on a wild scheme to rescue her father, who they all believed had deserted them. They came because she could lay claim to the shell throne, and because of that they would willingly lay down their lives for her. She owed them so much. She scraped back her chair and stood up.

'I just want to say thank you,' Taggie announced to everyone in a wavery voice. 'And tomorrow, if things start to go wrong, or look impossible, I want you to know I won't be stupid and just carry on regardless, even though it's my father who's in the dungeon. He knew the responsibility that would fall upon me one day, and did his best to protect me until I was ready. Getting captured by the Karrak Lords now would be a betrayal of all his hopes, of everything he did. And I believe he knows that. Thank you.'

'Well said, my dear,' Mrs Veroomes said. 'Yes, well said indeed.' She raised a small glass of red wine.

Sophie gave Taggie a big hug. 'You know that your comfort reaches all those who dream in the First Realm, don't you?'

'Yes.'

'Then remember this. Last night, your father will have felt your touch. He will know you're alive, and that you're here. He knows, Taggie, he knows. Imagine how happy he is knowing you're safe.'

'I never thought of that,' Taggie said. 'You're right. Oh, I wonder if I can find him in my dreams tonight.'

'Well it's about time you found out, if you don't mind me saying so, Majesty,' Wenuthi Jones said. 'You need to sleep. It's been a long day, and tomorrow will be even longer.' He scowled at the ceiling. 'Not that we will know daylight again, until you regain the throne.'

20

A QUIET AMBUSH

A hand shaking Taggie's shoulder woke her.

'Apologies, Majesty,' Wenuthi Jones whispered. 'But a posse of Ethanu has been sighted coming this way. Mrs Veroomes kept vigil all night, and saw them less than an hour ago. Piadrow took several members from his flock to check. They found the Ethanu about three miles away on the main road. They'll be here soon.'

Taggie groaned. It seemed like she'd only fallen asleep a few seconds ago. Yet she remembered dreaming again, comforting so many who cowered against the night which was pressing down on them. She had tried to find her father, but amid the multitude seeking her comfort it was impossible.

'Let's go,' Taggie said.

Wenuthi Jones planned the ambush carefully. The Authbourne Road came into Barrowden over a bridge that spanned the canal. There were burned-out cottages on either side, where he positioned his rangers. Piadrow and his flock waited high above, hidden by the thick snow. If everything was timed right, the posse of Ethanu would be caged in and unable to escape.

Taggie waited in one of the cottages, along with Rutubi Gorden, and Jakolb Smith, two of Wenuthi's most trusted Dolvoki Rangers. She watched as they prepared their shields, rubbing them as they would a beloved pet, and chanting small waking spells to the original invocations which lay inside the metal.

'Do they protect you?' she asked as little ribbons of scarlet light slithered round the metal like fast glow-worms.

'Why yes, Majesty,' Rutubi Gorden said. 'This shield belonged to my great-great-great-grandsire. A mage made it for him during the goblin war of the Yanrath Mountains, and it has protected our family from bad magic ever since. We rangers might not be mages, but this shield can withstand all but the strongest of their wretched death spells while we get close enough to give them a taste of our swords and axes.'

Taggie eyed the age-worn circle, noting several little blackened pockmarks across the surface. In her mind she recalled the enchantments of reinforcement. 'May I?' she asked.

'My lady,' he said solemnly, and held the shield out to her.

Taggie stroked it gently. The charmsward bands spun around, hammer aligning with lightning, diamond with the sun. '*Corrathi-dui*,' she murmured. The whole shield lit up with a purple glow, which quickly sank down into the metal.

Rutubi Gorden took the shield back, looking at it with wonder. 'It has never felt so strong before. Thank you, Majesty.'

Jakolb Smith cleared his throat. 'Um, your Majesty . . .'

'Of course.' Taggie beckoned him closer and renewed the protective invocations entwined with the sturdy metal of his shield.

'Thank you, my Queen-to-be,' he said gratefully.

Taggie then spun the tightest wardveil she could around them while they sat shivering in the cold, waiting.

The Ethanu were barely visible as they came over the bridge. In the few glimmers of light which penetrated the snowfall, Taggie saw six dark riders. They were nearly between the cottages when the leader stopped and held up his arm. The posse halted, waiting obediently. Peeping through a crack in the blackened stone wall, Taggie could just make out the shape of their trilby hats against the ghostly clouds. Steel-rimmed glasses gleamed a dull orange below the rims as the leader's head turned smoothly from side to side. His gaze swept over the broken walls and skeletal roofs, examining them slowly and carefully.

I haven't got the wardveil right, Taggie thought to herself. *I've blown it. They must know we're here.*

When the Ethanu leader's gaze reached the section of wall Taggie was crouched behind, it stopped. She sucked in her lower lip; the little symbols on the charmsward emitted the weakest maroon light as the wardveil tightened around her. 'Please, please,' she murmured.

The Ethanu leader urged his horse forward and they began to move on.

Taggie let out a long breath as quietly as she could. She wasn't surprised to find herself shaking.

'Now,' Wenuthi Jones shouted.

The rangers in both cottages sprang up, aiming their arrows at the Ethanu. Skyfolk descended out of the swirling snow, aiming more arrows.

'Surrender,' Wenuthi Jones demanded. 'And you will be spared.'

Taggie stood up behind the ranger chief. A dazzling blaze of violet light slashed out from the Ethanu leader, burning through the air towards her. Taggie was ready for him. She calmly held out her arm, palm up; the bands on the charmsward spun so fast they blurred, and the death spell burst apart, drenching the walls of the ruined cottage in a drizzle of tiny lightning bolts.

The rangers and skyfolk let loose their arrows. Scarlet and emerald flashes blossomed amid the Ethanu posse, but their enchantments shielded them, burning and breaking up the arrows before they reached their targets. More purple death spells flew out like miniature comets, and the rangers hurriedly brought up their shields. The enchanted metal protected them, but the blows against the mage-crafted shields were brutal, sending a couple of rangers staggering back.

Then the six horses were charging away from each other in different directions. Piadrow and another skyman dived down towards the leader as he galloped down the main road through the village. They stretched a slim rope between them: the leader rode straight into it and the rope caught him across his chest, sending him spinning backwards to crash on to the ground in a cloud of snow. Three more skyfolk landed around him, the glowing tips of their arrows pushing into his leather coat. He made one attempt to rise, but fell back on to the compacted snow, too dazed to resist further.

Two rangers brought down another Ethanu and a ferocious swordfight began. They had the advantage as he was unable to run, his stiff legs forcing him to stand his ground, though his sword arm moved with dangerous speed.

Felix scampered along the cottage wall and made a tremendous leap on to the back of a passing Ethanu. He held his shimmering green sword against the creature's neck. 'Dismount or die,' he said.

Taggie saw the Ethanu at the back of the posse galloping towards the bridge. Arrows fell smouldering around him; then he cast a shade and became almost impossible to see in the cold snowy gloom. She knew that if he made it over the bridge they'd struggle to find him out in the empty countryside. She pointed her finger at the bridge, yelling: '*Droiak!*' Her urgency powered the spell on its way. Pure white lightning flashed from her fingertip, and the middle of the bridge exploded. Even she was surprised at the power of the destruction spell. A huge fountain of bricks and stone and ice went hurtling high into the snowy night, causing the skyfolk chasing the Ethanu to scatter frantically. The Ethanu's shadecast broke, exposing a terrified horse at the edge of the bridge, rearing up on its hind legs to send its rider tumbling on to the snow.

Taggie was aware of Rutubi Gorden and Jakolb Smith gaping at her in astonishment. 'What?' she shrugged. 'He would have got away.'

'Few m-mages have your strength, Majesty,' Rutubi Gorden stammered.

'Oh?' She watched as the two rangers glanced at each other.

'No,' Jakolb blurted. 'None . . .'

'You are the Queen-to-be,' Wenuthi Jones said quickly as she strode over to them. 'It is to be expected.'

Rangers and skyfolk rounded up the vanquished Ethanu,

bringing them to the cottage where Wenuthi Jones was waiting. Taggie watched the posse approaching with that slow steady walk of theirs, just as they had in London. This time she wasn't in the least bit frightened – but she didn't trust them, even though the rangers had bound their wrists with enchanted cords. Something would have to be done about that.

Taggie let memories flutter through her mind, welcoming the warmer sunny ones of her grandmother, who had released a potent enchantment against the Rannalal knights on the only day they'd ever met. Five of the charmsward's bands whirred smoothly, aligning the symbols she sought.

For a brief moment the long-suffering village of Barrowden knew the touch of a summer sun and the scent of meadow flowers. As they entered the cottage, the apparition faded and the six Ethanu wilted into a deep dreamless sleep.

'It's not fair,' Jemima complained as she pulled an Ethanu's leather coat on over her *athrodene* mail. 'It itches like mad. And it smells, too.'

'How can it itch?' Taggie demanded. 'You're wearing armour underneath it.'

'It itches round my neck,' Jemima replied primly.

Taggie ignored her, and carried on buttoning up her own Ethanu coat. The effect of the wire-rimmed glasses was very odd: the world in front of her eyes had a purple and green tint. She used a draining enchantment, expelling the magic they contained until the lenses were just ordinary clear glass. With the trilby settled on her head, she checked herself out in the parlour mirror. Actually, the costume didn't look too bad, she decided. Shame the coat was so big on her.

'Aren't you a bit short for an Ethanu?' Sophie asked.

'I'll be on a horse,' Taggie answered defensively. 'And I'll cast a weak shading around myself – just enough to trick the eye. It'll be fine.'

'Please be careful, Majesty,' Mr Anatole said as he made a few adjustments to the way the coat hung. His hands trembled, and nothing he did seemed to make any difference. 'Overconfidence has brought down many fine ideals.'

'You can only be confident if you're not nervous,' Taggie told him quietly. 'And trust me, I'm very nervous.'

'Something we share, then, Majesty. But I am glad, for that will keep you alert.'

She smiled up at his concerned red face. 'Thank you, Mr Anatole. Without your support I doubt anyone would be helping me.'

He inclined his head. 'You are my Queen-to-be. Your wishes are all that matter.'

'I wish you were coming with us.'

'I would be a liability. These rangers are far more use in this endeavour than an old man of letters and law. But I will remain close, fear not.'

They trooped out into the inn's courtyard where the horses were waiting.

'I prepared this for you, my Queen-to-be,' Ronuld said anxiously as he thrust a package into her hands. 'Some food for the road. It's not much.'

'You always say that, yet it is always more than enough,' she told the kind innkeeper. 'Thank you for letting us stay.'

Taggie watched Mrs Veroomes help Jemima up on to one of the Ethanu's horses. 'Now remember,' said the old seer. 'The art is not something you can force. Be patient. Don't lose your temper.'

'I know,' Jemima said. She tipped her head forward, and the trilby fell across her eyes.

'Here,' said Mrs Veroomes, and unwound one of the purple and scarlet scarfs round her neck. She scrunched the square of silk up into a ball and stuffed it into the trilby. 'That should sit better.'

'Thank you,' Jemima said with a strong tremor in her voice.

'Be good. Stay safe.'

'I will.'

Sophie drifted over to Taggie as she was getting on her horse. 'Same goes for you,' she said. 'Be careful.'

'I'll be all right, don't worry,' Taggie said.

'I know.' The skymaid grinned. 'I saw the bridge explode.'

Taggie shuffled round in the big saddle until she was moderately comfortable. 'See you soon.'

'Yes,' Sophie said with a shrewd smile.

Taggie wondered what the skymaid was up to, and was about to ask when Wenuthi Jones called them to order and led them out of the inn's courtyard.

The four disguised rangers, along with Taggie and Jemima, made up the six-strong posse; Felix, who was now half Jemima's size, was riding with her and would hide under her coat once they approached the palace. Their 'captive' was Wenuthi Jones, whose horse was tethered to Jakolb Smith's: he would provide them with a reason for going down into the dungeons, hopefully without being questioned.

Four more Dolvoki Rangers and Mr Anatole were to ride with them for the first part of the short journey to the capital Lorothain, where they would venture into the city and try to make contact with the remnants of the palace guard.

Overhead flew Piadrow and fifteen of his flock, who would quietly spiral high above the palace during the rescue attempt, ready to dive down and pull the little party away to safety at a moment's notice.

Now that she was on her way, and surrounded by so many good people, Taggie finally allowed herself to feel some hope. 'We're coming, Daddy,' she whispered into the swirling snow. 'We're going to get you out of there.'

21

INTO THE DUNGEONS

Barrowden had been badly affected by the frost fungus, but Lorothain was in a much more advanced state of decay. Taggie could barely bring herself to look at it as they plodded steadily along the road beside the river Trambor, which circled the great city. She remembered the brief glimpse she'd enjoyed when they visited her grandmother's palace; then it had been a capital of fabulous towers, handsome chateaus, and long tree-lined boulevards, with sunlight glinting off a thousand crystal windows.

Now the spires were swamped by the saggy, dripping mushrooms. Several had already fallen under the weight, while more leaned precariously. The crystal was stained by putrid mats of grey and brown mould. Walls were encrusted with spiky growths of filthy icicles that seemed to be growing upwards out of the thick layer of snow smothering the avenues. An unhealthy cloud of smoke hung above the rooftops as people burned whatever they could to keep warm. And on top of it all, the snow continued to fall.

'I hope they'll be all right there,' Jemima said as they

watched Mr Anatole and the four rangers cross one of the bridges to the city wall.

'Where?' Felix's muffled voice came from inside her coat. 'I can't see a thing. And this Ethanu coat is making my fur itch.'

'They're on the bridge,' she whispered in annoyance. 'And shush in there! You'll get us caught.'

'Caught? Are there soldiers?'

'No! Not yet, anyway. We're fine. Now be quiet.'

The heavy bulge inside her coat shuffled round, then stopped.

Jemima looked along the bridge, past the wide open gates at the far end. The only things she could see moving along the city streets beyond were dark shapes which didn't look like any of the First Realm people they'd ever met. The eeriest thing was the lack of noise coming from the city, as if everyone was indoors asleep, or fearfully holding their breath.

At the end of every bridge, guarding the gateways into the city, stood a group of Rannalal guards. The disguised rangers kept on going, but Jemima couldn't help looking back just once to make sure Mr Anatole had got through. After a brief exchange with the guards, he disappeared under the archway and she let out a huge sigh of relief. He clearly hadn't been recognized, and the rangers accompanying him wore cloaks over their distinctive tunics.

*

It was another hour along the river road before they came to the wide greenway which led through the parkland to the palace. The oaks and cedars that lined it were smothered in bristly clumps of ice barbs. Tall metal posts rammed into the ground between each tree bore blazing torches, which cast a flickering orange light across the route. It revealed several squads of Rannalal and ordinary soldiers riding towards them. When Taggie looked round, she saw another Ethanu posse riding behind them. There was no backing out now.

Above them, an ominous hurricane-swirl of swollen slate-grey clouds spun slowly, barely higher than the palace turrets. At least they provided perfect cover for Piadrow and his flock.

Jakolb Smith urged his horse forward as they approached the huge outer gate in the palace wall. Thick stems of frost fungus had grown up the walls, looping round the arching gateway. Treacly liquids pulsed inside them, making them swing slowly from side to side.

A dozen Rannalal guards in their blood-red armour stood outside, along with some evil-looking six-legged hounds that snuffled and grunted at the approaching patrol. A single brazier burned to one side of the gates.

'Prisoner for questioning,' Jakolb Smith said in a low grumble.

'Where'd you find him?' one of the Rannalal asked in a gruff voice.

'Lurking in fields over by a village. He's a Dolvoki

Ranger by the clothes on him. Spying, I'll warrant.'

'They all do,' the Rannalal said. 'Treacherous scum.'

A gigantic man stamped out of the gatehouse. 'Take him to the Muraduku,' he grunted. 'That'll loosen his tongue soon enough.'

Jakolb Smith produced an unpleasant laugh. He tugged at the tether on Wenuthi Jones's horse. 'Come along, you filth. You heard what's to happen to you.'

Taggie didn't dare look round, didn't look down. She kept her back perfectly straight as they rode slowly under the gateway arch where the frost fungus dripped disgusting liquid on the icy ground. Every second she was expecting the shout to go up – a challenge that would bring a thousand armed creatures down upon them.

But then they were through and crossing the first

courtyard, where a few windows high above them glimmered orange. 'Where now?' she whispered to her sister.

Jemima shook her hand then opened it, studying the little rune stones on her palm. 'That way.' She pointed at another big arching gateway.

Jakolb Smith nodded softly, and nudged his horse towards it.

Sophie had waited all of twenty minutes after the rescue party left before slipping out of the inn's parlour, where two Dolvoki Rangers and a couple of skymen guarded the sleeping Ethanu prisoners. She pulled up the laces on the front of her grey tunic, tightening them against the frigid air, stuffed her floating hair under the cap, and checked her bow on its strap. Satisfied with her preparations, she stepped out into the courtyard, let her wings open wide, and took off into the clouds. Her little fists were held in front of her head, parting the big soft snowflakes as she flashed upward as fast as she could, leaving a thin, sparkling red contrail slowly fading away behind her.

No way was she going to miss out on the daring raid against the palace, no matter what she'd promised her father. She knew she could fly higher than most of her flock; all she had to do was keep above them out of harm's way. Her friends and family were putting themselves at tremendous risk for the First Realm, and it simply wasn't in her nature to wait behind. Being there to help in whatever tiny way she could was worth enduring her father's anger.

After a minute of hurtling straight up, she burst out of the top of the snow clouds into clean air. Up here, the moonclouds wrapped tightly around the sun shone a feeble cold radiance across the First Realm. She hated seeing it like this, with most of the lands and seas choking below the thick winter clouds.

Several miles away, a dense circle of spinning cloud rose up like a lone puffy mountain. She knew that it had to be squatting over Lorothain, casting the darkest shadow of all over the palace where Lord Jothran and his kind practised their terrible wizardry. Sophie altered course, curving round to line up on the very peak of the grisly mountain ahead.

Taggie and the rescue party dismounted at the far end of the third courtyard. It was a small square with high walls; the only light came from torches burning in three of the archways.

Ahead of them, at the foot of the wall, were steps leading down into the warren of vaults and cellars beneath the palace. Jakolb Smith led the way down into utter darkness.

'Who's there?' a voice demanded from the bottom of the stairs. 'Why are you here?'

'We bring a prisoner to the Muraduku,' Jakolb Smith said.

'This is not the Muradu—'

The voice was silenced by the sound of a fist striking a

face. There was a groan, then a thud of a body collapsing on to the ground.

'Curse the angels, I can see nothing down here,' Jakolb Smith complained.

Taggie recalled very clearly a spell to cast light, but she was afraid to utter the invocation. If the rest of her magical ability was anything to go by, it would be like switching on a searchlight. She came halfway down the steps and fished her torch out of a pocket. Its weak yellow beam flickered on, revealing a door that was covered in grey-green frost-fungus toadstools. She could see Jakolb Smith was bending over the unconscious body of the guard, and then the beam died. No amount of smacking the torch in annoyance or winding the handle could bring it back.

'Bad magic,' Taggie muttered. She could smell it in the air, a sour presence that clung to the walls of the palace like static electricity.

Felix squirmed out of Jemima's coat, shaking his matted fur out. His head bobbed round, taking in the ominous courtyard. 'I may be able to help.' He scampered down the steps past Taggie, growing in size as he went. A tiny spark of gold glowed at the bottom beside the door. 'Your grandmother's gift.' The squirrel was holding up his paw, and the gold light shone out of his ring.

A moment later, the rescue party was inside the cellar, and shedding their Ethanu clothing. They were in a long corridor with a curving brick roof. Twenty yards away, the walls glowed with a sickly blue-green light.

'Frost fungus,' Wenuthi Jones announced in disgust as he inspected the long fur-like patches creeping up the walls. 'But for once it's helpful to us.' He turned to Jemima. 'Blossom Princess?'

She took the rune stones out and threw them lightly on to the ground. They rolled forward and stopped. 'Straight on for a hundred metres,' she said.

It was a confident voice, Taggie thought, if you didn't know Jemima and her bravado. But she kept quiet, not wanting to upset her sister's concentration.

The party moved down the wide corridor, swords drawn, until they reached a junction of five corridors that looked identical.

Jemima stood in the middle and threw her runes again. The little stones rolled across the ancient flagstones, picking up speed and curving round so they skittered into the second corridor on the left.

'This way,' Jemima said in a chirpy voice, and gathered the runes up again.

Taggie had to admit, her sister seemed to know what she was doing.

As they entered the new corridor, Wenuthi Jones reached up and made a small chalk mark on the ceiling. While they had every hope Jemima could lead them to her father, there was no way of telling if she could see their way out again. Mrs Veroomes had been most evasive about that, so it was agreed they would mark their route.

The corridor went on for fifty paces. It ended in a

junction with three other corridors. Once more, Jemima threw the runes, which rolled down the right-hand fork.

There were doors all along this corridor: thick, heavy wooden squares that looked as if they hadn't been opened for a century. Iron torches were fixed to the walls, rusty now and also unused for an age. Thin strands of luminous frost fungus were beginning to engulf the iron.

Another junction: Jemima threw the runes again, and they descended a long flight of steps that led deeper below the palace.

Sophie reached the pinnacle of the cloud mountain, panting hard from the struggle. She didn't think she'd ever been so high before, but her size just made it possible: she was strong enough to lift herself further than any of the heavier adult skyfolk could. The air churned and groaned all around her as the clouds spun below, throwing her about like a twig on a whitewater stream. It was a scary place to be: all alone, and directly overhead the palace. The fact her father and his flock were close by didn't make it any easier.

When she looked down, she could see right into the heart of the cloud mountain, the calm eye of the storm. Except it was more like a cloud volcano, with a wide opening at the top and a deep central hole of clear air. Lightning flared around the twisting walls of the empty eye. Sophie imagined this is what it would be like looking through Mirlyn's Gate into the Dark Universe itself.

Lightning flashed again, sending long dazzling forks

licking around the cloud. Blasts of wild air knocked her about. But she'd seen something in there – something gliding around in that vast cylinder of clear air. A dark speck.

Sophie beat her wings as hard as she could, teeth clenched against the effort. She picked up speed, which made her flight a lot more stable. The lightning flared once more, and she squinted down.

There!

Three dark shapes at least a mile below her, just skirting the curving cliff-wall of cloud. It was all she could do not to yell out in fright. Every skychild knew that wing-shape. It was almost the first thing they learned. Parents taught it to them long before they even flew for the first time.

'Oh no,' Sophie moaned fearfully. 'No, no, no.'

A pack of rathwai, the Karrak Lords' deadly air hounds, were stalking the sky above the palace.

22

THE RESCUE

Jemima threw the runes for what must have been the twentieth time. The black stones bounced and rolled across the ground, then trundled off down a passageway that was lower and narrower than any they'd been following. The far end glowed with a bright orange light that contrasted with the cold, dim glow of the frost fungus.

She stared at it, not needing the runes any more. 'He's there,' she said faintly. 'Oh Taggie, he's just at the end of this corridor. Daddy's there. And he's alive.'

Taggie took an eager step forward. Wenuthi Jones put out an arm to stop her going any further.

'Majesty,' he said quietly. 'That is torchlight up ahead. And there will be guards. This is our part now. Let us play it to the full. Stay back, please.'

Taggie nodded reluctantly. She stood to one side as the five Dolvoki Rangers crept along the phosphorescent passage, their swords drawn.

Sophie flew around the vast crater in the cloud once more. So far she'd counted eight of the hideous rathwai circling slowly in the eye of the great storm. She couldn't be certain, but she thought there were more. They had slithered in and out of the cloud wall with its perilous ripples of lightning, making it difficult for her to count them.

Eight or eight hundred, it made no difference: Sophie's father was below the rathwai, hiding in the cloud just above the palace, completely unaware of the doom lurking above him.

As she watched the purposeful flight of the big savage beasts in the clear air below, she realized this was a well-planned ambush. They were waiting, just like her father. And when they pounced unseen from above, her father and the flock would stand no chance. Taggie's mission to rescue Prince Dino would also be over, the Queen-to-be probably captured.

They must be warned, Sophie told herself. That was all there was to it.

Sophie took out the alarm whistle which all of her kind carried in their tunics, and put it in her mouth, ready to blow. She stilled her wings as she passed over the clear air at the very centre of the cloud mountain. For a long minute she fell in silence, feet first, down and down into the awesome eye of the storm, arms outstretched as the air whipped past; then she flipped over. With her fists clenched in front of her so they pointed at the hidden ground, she began to fly once more, her body trembling at the exertion as her straining wings forced the stubborn air to part for her.

The shocking shapes of the rathwai grew larger and

larger as she power-dived fearlessly towards them, trailing a sparkling red contrail as she descended. Lightning crackled all around. She hadn't realized how big the rathwai really were, how sharp and cruel their beaks, how long and deadly their talons. And as she drew closer she saw that each one was being ridden by a Karrak Lord.

As she plummeted past them, a bewilderingly fast shooting star, she blew the whistle with all her might.

Sheer surprise froze the rathwai and their brutal masters for a moment. The piercing shriek of the skyfolk alarm whistle sounded clear and pure above even the thunderclaps that grumbled around. Then they saw her, plunging towards the bustling clouds at the base of the eye. Cries of hatred and outrage reverberated between the riders. One by one, the rathwai folded their wings and hurtled down after her, their talons spread wide, ready to tear her from the air. Death spells like small orange-and-turquoise comets were hurled after her by the Karrak Lords. She twisted and spun to dodge them, laughing in defiance as the deadly wizard light burned the sky around her. Then she was among the thick buffeting clouds of the storm at the base of the eye, and everything was black and cold.

For over half an hour, Piadrow and his companions had flown in a wide circle, taking it in turns to dip into the wispy fringe of cloud that made up the belly of the giant unnatural spiral poised above the palace. Each time, they had returned to report that there was nothing to see, and that the guards at the gates and those walking the battlements were unaware of the rescue mission. Piadrow himself had seen the six horses left tethered to railings in one of the inner courtyards. All seemed to be going well.

Piadrow signalled for his friends to gather round, and they hovered close by in the icy cloud as snow swirled past them. 'It shouldn't be much longer,' he told them. 'I want someone watching the palace permanently now. None of the guards are watching the clouds. We should be able to lurk safely amid the snow.'

'What part of the palace should we watch?' asked a skyman.

Piadrow was about to answer when he heard the alarm whistle. It was muffled by the cloud and the snow, but for all skyfolk of whatever flock, that sound was unmistakable. Even now, in the middle of a rescue mission, he couldn't afford to ignore it. 'Scatter and dive,' he ordered.

As he said this, he swooped down towards the palace below. Part of him wanted to wait to see who was blowing the whistle, and make sure the danger was real and not a trick. But he was above the heart of the Karrak Lords' domain in the First Realm; if there were going to be rathwai anywhere, it would be here. *How stupid*, he cursed himself silently. *We should have made sure.* As he soared towards the rooftops of the palace, there were shouts from below. Guards had heard the alarm whistle – they were looking upward now – searching the night sky for enemies.

Just then he caught sight of a slender red contrail bursting from the base of the cloud. It was a very familiar contrail, and it made his heart skip a beat in fright. 'Sophie?' he whispered. She produced a sparkle exactly like that when she powered her way along. He'd always been so proud of how fast his daughter was.

Two rathwai dropped out of the cloud right behind her. 'Sophie!' Piadrow bellowed. He launched himself straight at her, tugging his bow from its strap.

Three of his friends saw him turn round and head back up. They followed him, drawing their own bows.

A barrage of arrows fizzed extravagantly in flight and forced the rathwai to veer away. The Karrak Lords riding the beasts cast several death spells – Piadrow dodged frantically to avoid them.

'What are you doing?' he shouted at his daughter.

'I saw the rathwai,' Sophie called back through the snow. 'You had to be warned.'

Piadrow saw another two rathwai emerge from the clouds. 'How many are there?' he asked.

'At least eight,' Sophie told him.

'To the palace!' he called to his friends. 'Get down into the courtyards where they can't fly.'

Sophie needed no urging and zoomed downward. Piadrow followed her, with the rathwai in hungry pursuit.

As they flashed down past the top of the battlements, what looked like guard huts fell apart, revealing huge, squat crossbow-like devices. Soldiers swung them round on their heavy mounts. Large missiles were flung up into the air, attached to nets which spread wide behind them.

'They must have known we'd come for the prince,' Piadrow said in a shaken voice. Above him a dozen nets sailed across the courtyard, forming a cage roof between the battlements. None of the skyfolk would be able to get out now. 'The swine were ready for us.'

He landed close to the rescue party's horses. Torches

flared along the walls above him, bright flames sending out a sickly yellow light. Four more skyfolk landed in the same courtyard and hurried over to Piadrow and Sophie. High above the nets, rathwai cruised around the palace towers, squawking in dismay at having been cheated out of their prey.

Then the courtyard echoed to the sound of gates being slammed open. Soldiers began to march in.

Piadrow glanced down the staircase to the cellars. 'Warn the Queen-to-be,' he told Sophie quietly. 'Go quickly, now. All is not yet lost. We'll hold them off here as long as we can.'

Sophie hurried down the steps and through the door at the bottom, closing it quietly. She fluttered a few inches off the floor as her eyes grew accustomed to the eerie glow of the luminous frost fungus, then started off down the corridor. At the first junction she found the chalk mark, and quickly followed the trail.

There were four guards outside Prince Dino's cell. Skilled soldiers, they fought furiously against the rangers, refusing to back down. Swords slashed and parried in the flickering torchlight. There was little room with eight men battling together between the walls. They shouted and snarled at each other. Blades frequently struck the brick walls.

The horrible clash of weapons went on for what seemed like an age. But eventually the rangers triumphed and the last guard standing threw down his sword. His three injured comrades were held fast, swords at their throats, while rangers bound their hands.

'What is going on?' a shaken voice demanded from behind the iron door. 'Nicola? Nicola, is that you? Are the girls safe?'

'Daddy?' Jemima shouted, running forward.

'Jemima?'

'Daddy. It's me. Yes, it's me.'

'Oh no! What are you doing here? Where's your mother?'

Felix took a ring of keys from one of the guards, and unlocked the door. Jemima shoved it open and ran into the cell. Her father was standing there, an incredulous expression on his face. He sank to his knees and opened his arms wide. Jemima ran straight into the embrace.

'This is madness,' he cried, hugging her tight. 'You shouldn't have come.'

'You never told us about the First Realm, Daddy,' Taggie said, fighting back tears. 'Why didn't you tell us?'

'My darling,' he said, and gripped Taggie, holding both his daughters tight to him. 'I would have done; I would have told you all about the realms when the time was right. I really would. But you're so young.'

Taggie didn't care. *I've got my dad back*, she thought in amazement. His clothes were torn, there was dried blood on his face and arms, and his glasses were cracked. But that didn't matter. *We're together, and that's the important thing*.

'Majesty,' Wenuthi Jones said urgently.

'Yes?' Dino and Taggie said together.

Taggie gave her father a shy, awkward glance. She blushed, and dropped her gaze to the floor. 'Sorry.'

Dad hugged her for a long moment, and kissed the top of her head. 'It's OK,' he said. 'I know you dreamed. I felt your comfort while I slept, and it was fabulous. You are indeed the Queen-to-be.'

Taggie had to wipe tears from her eyes. 'You're not cross?'

'All I am is proud, my darling. That's all I've ever been.'

'I helped so many people,' she said eagerly. 'It was wonderful to do that.'

'Long live the Queen-to-be,' he said happily, then glanced round the corridor. 'Where's your mother?'

'Back home,' Taggie said, slightly bewildered by the question.

'I told you to go to her – she was supposed keep you safe.'

'We came after you, Daddy. We had to rescue you.'

'Please,' Wenuthi Jones said. 'Prince Dino, we must leave. Now.'

'Of course,' Dad replied, and gripped the ranger chief's arm. 'Is your army battling the dark forces in the palace?'

'No, Dad,' Taggie said. 'There's no army. It's just us.'

'We have arranged a safe route away from here,' Felix said. 'Fear not, Prince.'

'You brought my children on a rescue mission?' Dad asked with growing anger.

'I was the only one who could find you,' Jemima said. 'Don't be cross, Daddy, please. I'm a seer now. Mrs Veroomes is teaching me, just like you said in your letter.'

'All right,' he said with a sigh. 'Let's just get out of here, shall we?'

'Yes, sire,' Wenuthi Jones said.

The rangers shoved the guards into the cell and locked the door. The ranger chief took a step towards the passage and then stopped. A breeze blew against his face, making him frown. The torches on the wall flickered.

Something at the far end of the passage was sparkling red – it expanded rapidly and shot out in front of them. Sophie appeared, hovering beside Taggie. 'It's a trap,' she shouted frantically. 'The rathwai were waiting for us. We can't fly you out.'

Before Taggie could answer, the corridor was filled with harsh scraping noises. The metal doors of every cell were slowly opening.

23

TO THE HEART OF THE PALACE

'Run!' Wenuthi Jones cried.

Taggie didn't need to be told twice. She pelted down the passage with Jemima on her heels. She was frightened, yes, but mixed in with that fright was a boiling anger. All she seemed to do was run away – even now when she thought they'd finally gained the upper hand.

'They're coming,' Felix said.

Taggie risked a glance over her shoulder. Wenuthi Jones was bringing up the rear of the rescue party. Fifteen metres behind him the passage was completely filled with Ethanu, advancing with their slow unstoppable walk. Eerie orange light shone from their wire-rimmed spectacles, as if their eyes were on fire.

Taggie raised her hand. 'Duck!' she commanded.

Wenuthi didn't need any further instruction. He hit the ground fast. Dad was just giving her a puzzled look. Felix pulled him over.

'*Droiak!*'

The dazzling burst of light from Taggie's finger struck the roof of the passage. An avalanche of broken brick and chunks of rock came tumbling down. A thick wave of dust billowed along in front of it.

The rescue party stumbled on, coughing and wheezing until they reached some clear air at the next junction. There were six corridors leading away from it.

Dad stared at Taggie open-mouthed. 'When did you learn to do that?'

Taggie gave him a bashful shrug. 'You gave me the charmsward,' she said.

'Yes,' he agreed. 'But your strength . . .' he twitched his lips in a reluctant smile. 'Well done.'

Wenuthi Jones was just heading into the corridor with the chalk mark when he stopped. At the far end he saw the orange glimmer of torch flames. As the rescue party looked round, three more of the corridors had torches moving along them. Shouts and clattering armour were echoing from them.

'Princess, which way?' Wenuthi Jones asked.

Jemima's face was scrunched up in misery. She stared at the runes in her hand, close to tears. 'I don't know. Where do you want us to be?'

'Just take us away from the ambush,' Taggie said, trying to keep the panic from her voice.

'But they're everywhere,' Jemima said wretchedly.

'It's all right, my darling,' Dad said. 'Can you see where they *aren't* waiting for us? Take your time, now.'

Jemima glanced round the junction, then shut her eyes and took a determined breath. She pointed down one of the black stone corridors. 'This way.'

'Then that's the way we'll go,' Dad said warmly.

Taggie stood in the junction as the others dashed after Jemima and Dad. The torches in one of the corridors now revealed an approaching horde of gnomes riding on rats. She squealed in disgust and pointed her hand.

'*Droiak!*'

More chunks of rock came tumbling down, obliterating the gnomes and rats. She turned to the next corridor. Amid its darkness, small orange circles advanced inexorably.

'*Droiak!*'

The third passage.

'*Droiak! . . . Droiak! . . . Droiak!*'

The little junction was filled with cloying clouds of dust as she brought all but one of the corridors down with her destruction spell.

'That should stop them for a while,' she coughed as she jogged after the others.

At the next junction, Jemima sensed soldiers approaching along only two of the passages. They hurried into an empty one, which led them to a choice of just one clear passageway. Taggie brought down the whole junction behind them.

'Where now?' Taggie asked Wenuthi as they hurried along yet another stone-lined corridor.

The ranger chief's anxious eyes peered out of his dust-caked face. 'I'm not sure, Majesty. Perhaps if we can shake off our pursuers, an escape route might be found. But for now we have to stay ahead of them.'

'Exactly what was the plan?' Dad asked.

'We just wanted to get you out,' Taggie said. 'After that, I don't know. I didn't want to summon an army and go to war, which everyone wants me to do. So many people would be killed. I was hoping you'd know what to do instead. Mr Anatole said I had to sit on the throne, but he didn't know how to get me into the throne room. It's the best protected place in the First Realm, he said.'

'Yes . . .' her dad said slowly. 'It is.'

The next crossroads was a lot bigger than the previous ones. Prince Dino glanced around at the worn frescoes on the walls and grinned. 'I know where we are!' he cried, and headed straight for a set of stairs leading down.

'Are you sure?' Taggie asked. Down didn't seem to be the way they should be going to get out of the palace.

'Mr Anatole might be right,' Dad replied. 'The Karrak Lords cannot stand sunlight – at least not for very long. None of their kind from the Dark Universe can. If I could control the moonclouds properly, I could bring about a daylight which would last until they were forced to retreat back to whatever depths they came from. Without them, their followers – all the soldiers and spies and vermin who have flourished under their reign – would be lost.'

Taggie wondered why Dad had refused to come back and help the First Realm when Mr Anatole had first asked him to. He certainly sounded like a confident ruler.

There was no sound of pursuit as Prince Dino led them down the curving stairs. The furry strands of frost fungus hadn't reached this far. They were in complete darkness now. Felix held up his hand, and the ring shone with a pale gold light. The bottom of the stairs brought them out into a huge empty chamber with tall pillars around the walls. Two dozen tunnels led out of it, breathing a dry warm air gently over the little group.

'But, Dad,' Taggie said, looking round nervously. 'We can't get to the throne room. It would take an army to break through the walls at the centre of the palace.'

'You're quite right – it would,' her dad said in a voice that sounded suspiciously amused. 'But you're forgetting one thing.'

'What?' Jemima squeaked.

'I grew up in this palace. And there's nothing a boy likes to do more than explore. Especially the secret places . . .' He strode confidently across the chamber, leaving the others no choice but to follow. 'There is a way out beyond the palace walls from here that only Usrith's ancestors know of,' he said as he stopped by one of the mighty carved pillars. 'But there's also another route, one that will take me right into the throne room. I'm going to go there and sit on the shell throne, I am still a Prince of this Realm, and I have that right.'

'Yes, Daddy, you are a prince,' Taggie said calmly.

'Right then. Felix, Wenuthi, I'm entrusting you to take my daughters out to safety, please.'

'Yes, sire.'

'But I am the Queen-to-be,' Taggie said quietly; all her

disapproval of the title had vanished. '*I* serve the First Realm now.'

'Absolutely not. Taggie Paganuzzi, you will do as you're told and leave right now.'

'I have already directed the moonclouds, so I know I can do it.'

'When?' Dad snapped. 'Karrak wizardry controls the moonclouds now. Only the power of the shell throne itself can best them.'

'It was the day I saved you from the Rannalal knights. You were playing football with your friends in the palace gardens. Do you remember?'

Prince Dino swayed back as if she'd hit him. 'That was *you?*' he croaked in shock.

'I told you then that you would know who I was one day. Now you do.'

'But . . . how? That was seventy years ago.'

'The Great Gateway Arasath, sire,' Felix said. 'It was playing rogue that day, as it always delights in doing. It sent us back through time. I was there too, if you recall.'

'Yes . . . yes, the Weldowen, I do remember.' Prince Dino gave Jemima a forlorn look. 'And you, my darling Jem, you were there as well, weren't you?'

'Yes, Daddy.'

'I spent so long looking for you,' he said wearily to Taggie. 'So very long.'

'Well, now you've found me,' she replied with a smile. 'And I've discovered who and what I am because of it. I am the Queen-to-be. I have to sit on the shell throne, Daddy.'

'Yes.' Her father nodded, though he looked desperately unhappy. 'Yes, you do, my Queen.' He looked round the Dolvoki Rangers. 'May I have a sword? My magic is not strong – I will need something sharp to help protect my daughters.'

Wenuthi Jones handed him a sword he'd taken from one of the dungeon guards, bowing graciously.

'I thank all of you for coming to rescue me. Now we must do what we can for the rest of this realm. Our realm, which I was so foolish to leave.'

Prince Dino led them along the chamber to a pillar on the wall furthest from the stairs. '*Elraf*,' he said, and a rectangle of stone at the base of the pillar swung back silently.

Taggie followed her father into the tunnel beyond. It was only just high enough to stand up in, and so narrow they had to walk in single file. The light of Felix's ring was barely enough to stop her cracking her head on low snags of rock.

It must have taken them an hour to walk through the tunnels cut into the bedrock deep beneath the palace. There were endless junctions and flights of stairs. Prince Dino never hesitated in guiding them, but by the end, Taggie was starting to feel the weight of rock pressing in around her. She longed for wide spaces and light.

At the foot of the final staircase, Prince Dino gathered them around. 'The throne room has three doors,' he told them. 'All are big and ancient – they're part of the original castle, so they have sturdy bolts as thick as my leg, and are saturated with shielding enchantments. If we can close these doors, we should have a little time before the Karraks and their followers can break through. Hopefully enough time for Taggie to sit on the shell throne and open the moonclouds wide.'

'There will be guards,' Taggie said. 'There have to be.'

'Yes there will, but the cellars and dungeons are being searched as everyone hunts for us. And there are enough passages and vaults down here to swallow up entire armies. I'm hoping the remaining guards will be *outside* the doors to prevent us getting in,' Dad said, and held up his new sword. 'If not, the rangers and I will take care of them while you run for the shell throne – that's all that matters now.'

'What if it doesn't open for me?' Taggie asked, suddenly anxious.

'Taggie, darling . . .' He gave her a kiss on the forehead. 'The shell throne will open for you. I promise. Now, are you ready?'

'Yes.'

They started up the last stairs, curving round and round in a spiral. At the top, Felix covered the ring with his paw. In the pitch black, she could hear her father whisper an enchantment, and a section of the smooth stone wall swung open.

Taggie knew the throne room well enough from her

dreams. It was circular, with a black-and-white marble floor. Raised on a dais, the ancient shell throne itself faced the three doors. Benches filled tall alcoves around the walls, so courtiers could sit while the Queen received her guests.

It was one of those alcoves that served as a hidden door to the secret stairs. Prince Dino and Felix emerged first, looking round cautiously. It was almost as dark in the throne room as it was at the top of the stairs. None of the lightstones in the huge candelabras hanging from the ceiling had been lit. Above them, a feeble grey light seeped through the wide smears of frost fungus that grew across the domed crystal roof. Shadows ruled the circular chamber, smothering the walls and absorbing all sound. Taggie could barely see her own feet on the floor, let alone the dais with the shell throne. Her boot made a soft squelch as she stepped forward. She suspected it was yet more frost fungus – the air certainly reeked of it.

The three main doors were just visible fifty paces to her left; ghostly arches amid the black shadows. All the hairs on her spine pricked up. The dark enchantments that swarmed through this part of the palace were thick and oppressive.

Now she could make out the tall doors, she knew roughly where the shell throne was. Her father's hand closed on her arm. 'I don't think there are any guards,' he whispered into her ear. 'You go for the throne. We'll get the doors.'

Taggie nodded before she realized how useless that was in the dark. She started walking carefully across the marble flooring, wincing every time she put her boot down on another strand of squishy frost fungus. Her heart was racing at the prospect of sitting on the throne. She thought about how the peoples of the First Realm would welcome the uncaging of the sun; how they would rejoice.

'You see, brother,' Lord Golzoth's voice said from the thick shadows. 'I told you if we just waited, she would come to us.'

24

THE THRONE ROOM

Taggie spun round, her arm lashing out. '*Droiak!*'

The spear of lightning which was her destruction spell shattered against Lord Golzoth's protective enchantments, forming a web of little glaring tendrils that screeched harmlessly around his smoke cloak. Even so, he swayed backwards from the force of the spell.

Taggie gasped in surprise. The Karrak Lord was hanging upside down from an alcove, with long bony toes just visible above the hem of his cloak as they gripped at the carvings along the top. He let go, and flipped round in the air to land in a crouch. 'You're a strong little thing, aren't you?' His hand rose, and a neon-blue light streaked down his slender arm to burst from his fingers. The death spell broke apart on the shield Taggie spun around herself, but she felt her boots slide back several centimetres across the floor as it struck.

'Where does that strength come from, I wonder?' Golzoth continued. 'Certainly not this feeble clown, Prince Dino. Your grandmother, perhaps?'

'Does it matter?' another voice asked from behind the shell throne. The shadows began to withdraw from the alcoves, and Taggie let out a groan of utter dismay. Karrak Lords and Ladies were hanging upside down in every alcove.

One by one, they began to lower themselves to the floor. The smoke cloaks of the Lords swirled as they righted themselves, while the silver mist the Ladies wove around themselves flowed like gowns of mercury. The Dolvoki Rangers held their shields up resolutely as they closed in a protective circle around Sophie and Jemima. Taggie stood next to her father, staring at the tallest Karrak Lord, the one she knew must be Jothran. The hood of his smoke cloak flowed back as he tipped his head to one side in order to study her. Like his brother, Lord Golzoth, his sickly-white skin was drawn so tightly over his head he looked like an animated skull. Wrap-around sunglasses were perched on his blade-like nose, with its single nostril flaring as if he was sniffing her scent.

The hem of his cloak swished about, licking the marble tiles as he slithered forward. When he reached the shell throne, he parted his milky lips to show off pointed silver teeth.

'I'm impressed, Queen-not-to-be,' he said in a sarcastic purr. 'Using treachery and deception to get into the palace, then sneaking through secret passages to steal what you desire. You're clearly learning the new ways of this realm. Too bad you tried to use them against me. You had so few options, they were all very predictable. I doubted that anyone would be so stupid as to try and rescue Prince Dino from my dungeon, but Golzoth convinced me you were just as weak as the deluded and disgraced Lord Colgath. Hard to believe, but he was right – as always.'

'My pleasure to serve, brother,' Golzoth said slickly as he glided over to Jothran's side.

The Karrak Lords and Ladies had completely encircled Taggie and the desperate rangers. There must have been at least twenty of them, she thought. Torches flared in the long cloisters beyond the throne-room doors, revealing columns of soldiers led by Ethanu officers heading towards them.

'What do you want?' Taggie demanded.

'Oh I think you know that, my dear Queen-not-to-be,' Jothran said. A forlorn green light trickled down his long fingers as he held his arm out. Then it dripped down to spread little phosphorescent streams over a stone altar that had been set up next to the shell throne. As it was revealed, Taggie heard Jemima whimper in terror behind her.

Taggie stared defiantly at the King of Night. 'Is that the best light you can conjure up? Let's take a better look, shall we?' She tipped her head back and snarled at the black clouds swirling above the palace. Deep inside herself she could feel magic building; it was different to the enchantments and spells.of her ancestors in the charmsward. This was powered by her fright and anger. It was her own magic, and it yearned to be free. She let it loose. 'Go away!' she yelled furiously at the storm.

*

In the city of Lorothain, people knew something important was happening. They could hear it in the new creaking of the mighty storm that spun overhead. They heard it in the angry cries of the rathwai that came diving out of the clouds and snow. They saw it in the sizzling lightning that snapped down to strike the towers of the palace.

At first they peered out of their windows and saw squads of soldiers belonging to the King of Night marching hurriedly along the streets. It was like watching ants from a nest that had been kicked over.

Braver residents started to venture outside, wrapped up against the dark and cold. They stood pressed against the walls of their homes as the soldiers marched past in the snow. It was clear to all that the self-proclaimed King of Night was calling his forces to him. Nobody was left to impose his authority on the city's population.

More people began to emerge from their houses. Questions were whispered along the streets and boulevards and frozen canals. 'What has happened?' They asked one another. 'What has upset the King of Night?'

'The usurper fears the Queen-to-be,' a single gurgling voice declared in the middle of the central market square.

The nervous crowd turned to see a tall old Shadarain dressed in the striking robes of the royal palace. He was standing on a cart, surrounded by men in the unmistakable tunic of the Dolvoki Rangers. Around the cart a squad of four-armed Holvans cast away their cloaks to show their palace guard armour.

'She is our Queen-to-be,' Mr Anatole declared passionately. His arm thrust out, pointing accusingly at the palace on the other side of the river. 'And that is *her* throne.'

The crowd roared its approval. Privately Mr Anatole was very worried that something had gone badly wrong. The Karrak Lords were clearly in disarray, but the skyfolk hadn't yet appeared carrying the rescue party to safety.

'If she needs help taking it back, then I will gladly give her that help. I ask all of those here today to join me.' He jumped down from the cart and walked purposefully towards the broad boulevard leading out of the market square, and towards the Majpan Bridge, which was closest to the palace. The Dolvoki Rangers and palace guard fell in around him. Then the crowd surged along, following them and cheering wildly. Mr Anatole was heartened by the heavy thudding footfalls of trolls among them. A surprising number of people were carrying weapons; swords and daggers and shields were held up and shaken defiantly at the storm overhead as they marched along to challenge the King of Night.

Above the palace, the entire cloud mountain writhed in torment as Taggie's cloudbuster magic reached it. Huge blasts of wind rose from nowhere and tore the entire swirling mass to shreds.

Far, far above, a single tiny crack appeared amid the blackened moonclouds. A lone beam of sunlight streamed down.

It struck the crystal dome roof of the throne room. Frost fungus boiled, then burned. And the centre of the throne room was suddenly as bright as a summer's day.

The wild wailing of the Karrak Lords and Ladies was deafening as they cowered away from the vast column of sunlight beating down. Taggie and the rangers had to clamp their hands over their ears the noise was so piercing. She watched smoke cloaks foam and thicken to impenetrable black as the dark creatures shrank back against the walls. Silver gowns rippled with reflected sunlight as the Ladies twisted about in distress.

All of them had recoiled – apart from Jothran and Golzoth. They stood their ground as their cloaks grew dense, protecting them from the unwelcome light. The edge of the sunlight was barely metres from them, causing the matting of frost fungus on the floor to shrivel and smoulder.

'Is that the best you can do?' Lord Jothran taunted. 'A single sunbeam in a whole realm of night-shadow? *My* night.'

Taggie struggled to smile back at him. She'd expected the sunlight to send the Karraks fleeing from the throne room, allowing her to sit on the shell throne. Instead, the King of Night continued to stand between her and it as if nothing had happened. He was so strong that her very best spell left him unmoved.

'Strength,' she whispered. And there was Mr Koimosi, her own memory for once, scolding her as always that she must use her opponent's strength against them. She dived frantically into the charmsward's memories, searching for something she could use. There were so many memories, so many spells and enchantments. She had to find something. The whole First Realm depended on it. On *her*. There had to be something. Somewhere!

Mr Anatole was fifty metres from the Majpan Bridge. In front of him, the King of Night's soldiers were lining up in heavy ranks to stop Lorothain's citizen army from going any further. Ethanu officers barked sharp orders, and swords were drawn. Bows were stretched back. Arrows aimed. The sight of so many soldiers moving in unison with such deadly purpose was deeply intimidating.

Facing them through the soft snowfall, the first rank of men on either side of Mr Anatole raised their enchanted shields. The moment stretched out.

A violent wind rose from nowhere, driving the snow into both armies like a blast of thorns. Above them, the gigantic clouds were tumbling away. A slender sunbeam reached down through the expanding gap to touch the middle of the palace.

'Our Queen-to-be!' Mr Anatole howled.

'Our Queen,' came the almighty shout behind him. The army from Lorothain charged forward, and it was all Mr

Anatole could do to stay on his feet as he was swept along.

Arrows flew. The two armies slammed into each other, and swords and knives slashed and bit and stabbed. Mr Anatole was buffeted between fights, desperately trying to dodge swords swung by men from both sides.

'Rathwai!' the cry arose. 'Rathwai are coming.'

Mr Anatole looked up to see the vile creatures sinking out of the chaotic sky. Talons as big as him opened wide, ready to grab.

Twenty miles distant from Lorothain, Earl Maril'bo sat cross-legged, close to the edge of the Jaribal cliffs − a mile-high precipice that in better days gave a perfect view across the pretty countryside to the city. Today all that it revealed was darkness and dreary snow. He didn't bother looking at anything. His eyes were closed, allowing him to see inwards.

So it was that Earl Maril'bo waited patiently, his hands resting on his knees, palms upward. The members of his band were beside him, spread out along the top of the cliff, waiting in silence. Elves could wait for decades if they had to. Time wasn't as important to them as it was to mortal races of the realms.

Then somewhere in the darkness above, a crack appeared in the murky shell of moonclouds. A crack opened by a strange, foreign kind of magic. Sunlight fell on to the palace of the First Realm once again. Just a thin beam to be sure. But sunlight nevertheless.

Earl Maril'bo opened his eyes. 'Our Queen-to-be brings us light,' he said. As he rose, he pulled his mirror board off his back, and dropped it down on the snow at his feet.

The memories within the charmsward flashed through Taggie's mind. So many of them – so many ancestors offering up what they believed might help. She was far back through the generations now, and still she'd found nothing.

Around her in the throne room, the Karraks were recovering from the rush of light she had summoned. Lords and Ladies stood up proud again; then, ominously silent, they slid slowly towards the great column of sunlight that shone down on Taggie and the rescue party.

'What do we do?' Sophie asked desperately as her wings began to vibrate. Every strand of her red hair was stretching out around her head like a thick halo as she drew her dagger, ready to fight for the Queen-to-be.

'Use their strength against them,' Taggie told her. Right at the end of the charmsward's memories Usrith himself was waiting. Taggie saw him, old and frail, yet perfectly content as he stood beside the newly forged shell throne. It opened so that his daughter Lucithe could sit upon it. He smiled at his success, seeming to look directly at Taggie. And finally she remembered everything she needed.

Mr Koimosi would have been proud of her. She stared right at Lord Jothran. 'You want me?' she growled the challenge. 'Come and get me.'

'Taggie . . .' her father moaned in warning.

'I will be the next Queen of Dreams,' she said calmly. On her wrist, the charmsward bands were spinning quickly and smoothly. Each symbol glowed a proud and vibrant turquoise. Water aligning with rock, which aligned with the sun. Then came the triangle symbol clicking neatly into place. The infinity sign . . . 'Believe in me.'

'Oh but I don't,' Jothran told her. 'Brothers. Sisters. Together now.'

The eerie, quivering black-and-silver silhouettes of the Karraks glided to a halt surrounding the cylinder of sunlight. They raised their arms in unison to expose hands with ring-covered fingers that flexed like crab-legs. Twenty-seven immensely powerful death spells streamed out, each one aimed directly at Taggie.

The enormous strength of Karrak wizardry struck her, and the surge of magical energy was far greater than she expected, scorching her skin as it flooded across her. She cried out in pain. Her father steadied her before she could fall, but thanks to Usrith's guidance spell, the power flowed directly into the charmsward, causing the symbols to flare incandescently.

'Best you can do?' she asked Jothran in a shaky voice.

Jothran was now done toying with his prey. His mouth parted wide, and his sharp silver teeth lengthened into menacing fangs. 'Brothers, sisters – again!'

The death spells slammed into Taggie once more. She cried out at the top of her voice. This time she fell. The circle of sunlight on the black-and-white marble floor shrank. She couldn't lift her arm. The magic absorbed by the charmsward had a terrible weight all of its own. Each symbol shone with a poisonous orange light. Her skin blistered beneath the bands.

Jothran pressed home his advantage. The Karraks skated in closer as the sunlight contracted. Death spells were cast again.

Even though she'd been knocked to all fours, whimpering at the pain, Taggie caught sight of Lord Golzoth. He was frowning as if he suspected something wasn't quite right, turning away from his brothers and sisters.

'You weaken,' Jothran gloated at Taggie.

Taggie raised her head, and grinned at the King of Night, a grin that told him just how wrong he was. 'Actually, I don't. Thanks for the energy boost, I couldn't have done this without you.'

The charmsward bands spun. Six sun symbols lined up, each ablaze with pure white light. Taggie thrust her arm upward. There was no memory to follow – this was her own spell, and because Usrith understood how to shape raw magic, so did she. 'Burn hot,' she ordered the incredible power boiling inside the charmsward. 'And burn bright.'

25

SHINING LIGHT ON THE PROBLEM

All the magic in the death spells which the Karrak Lords and Ladies had flung at Taggie burst out of her charmsward at once, streaming up through the glass dome of the throne room and into the sky above. But now the power was shaped the way she wanted it.

The dense shroud of moonclouds held in place by Karrak wizardry scattered like minnows before a shark. A wonderful blaze of sunlight shone across the whole of the First Realm again. Then Taggie's spell poured into the very sun itself. It began to shine brighter and brighter.

In the throne room, the broad beam of light shining through the crystal roof started to expand rapidly, chasing the fleeing Karraks as the desperate Lords and Ladies flung themselves for the doors and whatever shade they could find.

There was none.

As the sunlight flooded into every part of the palace, it grew until it was such a powerful glare that even Taggie had to cover her eyes. Somewhere close by, she heard the cries of the stricken Karraks as the deadly light struck them. The horrible sounds of sizzling began.

Earl Maril'bo didn't shield his eyes from the new and splendid dawn. He smiled up at the amazing brilliance, opening his arms in greeting. 'Our Queen-to-be brings us rain,' he declared.

The snow that was falling all around began to melt under the intense light. Every flake turned to rain. Rainbows bloomed right across the First Realm. Thick, vivid rainbows that stretched from the ground right up to the top of the atmosphere, swirling and shimmering.

Earl Maril'bo jumped on to his mirror board, which went *swooshing* down the short icy slope. It shot out over the edge of the massive cliff, and sliced through the Realm-encircling rainbow, jetting out a spray of kaleidoscopic sparks in its wake.

Other members of his band followed him, ripping their way through the dazzling sky. Together they hurtled down towards the city of Lorothain that sprawled far below.

On the Majpan Bridge, it had been going badly for the ragtag Lorothain army. The rathwai fell mercilessly on the townspeople, yanking them up into the sky and sending them tumbling to crash brokenly on roofs and streets. Beaks the size of canoes snapped and crunched. The King of Night's soldiers poured into the gaps torn by the rathwai, taking advantage of the panic.

Mr Anatole was clubbed to the ground, where he lay grazed and bruised. Many boots stomped on him as the battle raged. One of the rathwai demolished a nearby building, sending a torrent of stone, timbers and slate pouring on to the street, crushing soldiers of both sides.

Then the moonclouds erupted. Light shone down, and Mr Anatole had to put up his arm to protect his eyes from the glorious white heat. The fighting stopped for a long wonderful minute, and awestruck silence claimed Lorothain.

Slowly the light shrank back to the brightness of a normal summer afternoon. Dazed soldiers began to look round as the snow turned to rain which pattered down on the frozen city.

Mr Anatole saw the soldiers gather themselves again. Those in the King of Night's army were turning to look anxiously at the palace. The revolting frost fungus that had spread across its walls and turrets was seething and evaporating, leaving behind layers of black soot.

Ethanu, who had nothing to lose, shouted harsh commands. The Lorothain army saw its hated oppressors bringing up their swords, and battle resumed in the vivid pouring rain. Mr Anatole tried crawling across the slippery snow as his sodden robes flapped around him. He managed to pick up a short sword from a dead soldier, and looked round at the men fighting so ferociously.

'Oh my Queen,' he groaned. 'This should not be.' He staggered up to his feet. 'She sits upon the throne,' he called amid the noise and fury and blood. No one listened to him. 'It is over.' One of the Ethanu was staring at him.

'Surrender,' Mr Anatole implored. 'Help stop this.'

The Ethanu raised an arm. Bright gold sunlight was reflected off his wire-rimmed glasses as he started chanting a death spell . . .

Then he was gone, snatched away into the sky by giant talons.

Mr Anatole gaped at the sight, not understanding. A second later he had to throw himself to the ground as another rathwai swooped down low. It had no Karrak Lord rider to direct it any more. More of the savage creatures started to attack the city. Enraged by the sunlight, the rathwai were going berserk, not caring who they killed.

Soldiers from both sides fought the rathwai as well as each other. The creatures attacked buildings, reducing them to rubble. Children cried in terror. Mr Anatole stumbled through the chaos. The huge battle descended into a madness from which nobody could escape.

'Elves!' went up the shout. 'The elves are coming.'

Mr Anatole looked up to see the amazing sight of an entire band of elves surfing along the colossal rainbow that filled the sky. Great sprays of glittering light fountained out from the back of their mirror boards as they zoomed forward. They began to pull firestars from their bandoliers, and sent them skimming through the colourful rain. The little discs expanded rapidly as they shot across the rooftops, turning into flaming circles that sliced into the rathwai. Earl Maril'bo's first shot decapitated one of the beasts, and its corpse crashed on to the frozen river

Trambor, smashing straight through the ice.

The elves curved gracefully through the air and flung another batch of firestars. The surviving rathwai flapped their leathery wings frantically, seeking to escape into the torrential downpour. Several more were brought down. Then the elves were surfing tight over the heads of the battling soldiers. They held curving blades in their fists, blades that slashed down to cut effortlessly through any enchantment shields the Ethanu attempted to spin.

With their officers decimated, ordinary soldiers of the King of Night threw down their weapons and finally surrendered. Amid huge cheers of welcome, the elves skidded down on to the ground. Bells were ringing right across the city to celebrate the liberation.

Mr Anatole was shaking from shock and surprise as Earl Maril'bo bounced his mirror board on the slippery ice of the boulevard in front of him. The huge elf smiled down at the sodden, battered old equerry. 'Dude, how's it hanging?'

Taggie risked taking her arm away from her face. It was still bright in the throne room, but not blindingly so. Around her, the Dolvoki Rangers were peering about with equal uncertainty.

A nasty brown vapour was rippling through the air. Jemima waved her hand in front of her nose in dismay. 'That really pongs,' she exclaimed.

'Price of victory,' Felix said in a voice that had no sorrow whatsoever.

Taggie eyed the oval mounds of smouldering ash that were scattered across the throne room floor. All of them were studded with sunglasses and gaudy rings. Beyond the three doors, in the great hallways of the palace, regiments of soldiers were slowly starting to glance round. When they saw the tarnished jewellery glinting amid the ash they understood exactly what had happened to their dark masters. Frightened eyes peered at her and her tiny escort of Dolvoki Rangers.

Their indecision wouldn't last long, Taggie knew, and there were an awful lot of them. The charmsward bands unlocked their six-sun combination – lining up doors with stone. '*Olzet*,' she murmured.

All three of the throne room doors slammed shut, the noise reverberating throughout the palace. Huge iron bolts slid across, sealing them securely.

'I was about to do that,' her father said.

'I know, Dad.'

He put his arms round both sisters, hugging them tight. 'You were utterly amazing. You know that, don't you?'

Taggie grinned up at him as a colossal feeling of relief swept through her. She didn't ever want him to let her go. 'Thanks, Dad.'

He kissed her brow, then took her and Jemima by the hand and walked towards the dais. As the three of them drew near, the pearl-white shell throne let out a soft creak. The upper half slowly hinged upward to reveal the purple and scarlet silk cushions.

Wenuthi Jones dropped to one knee; the rest of the rangers followed his example. Felix bowed low, his teeth chittering in excitement.

'Your throne and realm awaits, Queen-to-be,' Prince Dino said, and smiled encouragement. He looked melancholy and elated at the same time.

Taggie stared at the throne for a moment, suddenly frightened again by everything it resembled, everything she'd have to do for the rest of her life. 'Daddy . . . ?'

'Well, go on,' Jemima said impatiently. 'Sit on it. Honestly, Taggie!'

And Taggie was laughing at her sister. Then she took a breath and, still smiling, lowered herself on to the soft cushions of the shell throne of the First Realm.

'Long live the Queen of Dreams,' Prince Dino and the Blossom Princess said in unison.

Taggie beamed at them, and wiped away the moisture

welling up in the corner of her eye. This time it was the memories of the shell throne itself, not those of the charmsward, that bubbled through her mind: the grand coronations of Queens past, when the throne room was filled with the people of the First Realm dressed in their finest robes and gowns and uniforms. All through the Realm there had been day-long festivities and pageants and parties. Exalted guests from other Realms had attended the banquet after the ceremony. Every child had been handed a specially minted celebration coin. In all the Realm's cities, towns and villages, buildings were decked out in colourful flags and bunting. And there was music everywhere, with singers and minstrels and orchestras and bands playing non-stop so everybody could dance merrily. That was the grandiose way it always had been, making it the greatest day of every generation.

Taggie let out a long sigh, slightly sad that she hadn't come to the throne amid such a spectacle. But despite that, she knew she was now the Queen of Dreams – not just because who her parents were, but because she had earned it. That made everything worthwhile.

26

THE FLOWERS OF VICTORY

Two days later, Jemima, Felix and Mrs Veroomes were walking through the palace grounds. The sun shone warmly overhead and the snow and ice were melting away, making the ground slippery with slush. Even Jemima had to admit it had been an astonishing two days.

After Taggie and the others had spent three hours barricaded in the throne room, Mr Anatole had arrived at the palace, leading the elves along with most of Lorothain's residents. The King of Night's army had formally surrendered. They'd been disarmed, and taken down into the dungeons. All across the First Realm, the people who'd followed the Karrak Lords, believing their promises of profit and glory, melted away like the dwindling snow.

Towns and villages around the Great Gateways reported a huge number of creatures and people passing through, returning to wherever they'd come from. Courts were set up for the King of Night's soldiers, who received work sentences so they could usefully repair some of the damage they'd caused, before they were banished from the First Realm. A surprising number asked for permission to stay after their sentences finished, which Taggie granted.

Refugees who'd spent weeks and months hiding out in woods and caves returned home to joyful reunions with their neighbours. Everyone started stripping off the slimy remains of frost fungus from their homes, throwing it on to huge bonfires, whose meagre blue flames and putrid smoke lasted for months.

On the morning of the second day, Taggie and Jemima attended the mass funeral service for all those who'd perished at what was now known as the Battle of Majpan Bridge. The soldiers of both armies were buried alongside each other with full honours in a field beside the river. The only exception to the burial were the corpses of the rathwai, which were dragged away and burned in an old stone quarry.

After the funeral, the restoration of the palace began in earnest. Teams of builders and artisans arrived to strip out the foul fixtures which the Karraks had installed. They were aided by mages who dispelled the dark enchantments that still lingered in many of the artefacts before they could be safely taken down and destroyed. It was clear the renovation would take months, but Prince Dino was absorbed by the task, striding around and explaining how the whole place was to be restored to the splendour he remembered from his own childhood.

Jemima certainly couldn't complain at the suite of rooms traditionally occupied by the Blossom Princess. There would be maids and other staff, Dad promised, just as soon as things returned to normal; a timetable nobody was clear about. And besides, he pointed out, they were due back at Mum's in ten days. After that it would be the end of the summer holiday, and time to go back to school.

'School?' the sisters had bleated incredulously that morning at breakfast in the palace's sumptuous banqueting hall, which had a table long enough to seat a hundred people.

'But . . . but, I'm the Queen of Dreams!'

'And I'm the Blossom Princess!'

'And nobody in this realm wants uneducated people occupying the palace,' Dad replied. 'So school it is.'

'Quite true,' Mr Anatole had said as he helped himself to another slice of toast.

Taggie's mouth had dropped open in shock at that betrayal.

'Both of you are going back to school. End of discussion.'

'Dad, you're being so unfair.'

'Would you like to try and argue that with your mother?' he had asked calmly.

'No, Dad,' they had chorused, hanging their heads in dismay.

Passing trees that had lost their leaves, and bushes that were thawing out to resemble clumps of bare wire, Jemima finally found the big garden with the tree house where they'd met their grandmother that one and only time. It had survived the whole ordeal untouched, though its veranda was sagging a little and the windows now resembled sleepy eyes. She was glad about that, but her smile wasn't as broad as it should be. She sighed.

'What's the matter, Jem?' Felix asked.

'Nothing.'

His sharp little teeth chittered as if chewing an invisible nut, and he cocked his head to one side to study her.

'Well,' she admitted, 'it's just that Taggie's the Queen of Dreams now . . . Not that she doesn't deserve it,' she added hurriedly. For the last two days, the palace had been besieged by people from the nearby towns and villages; all of them desperate to see Taggie – to thank her, to discuss what was to be done next. To ask about the sun and the seasons. To offer help. They brought gifts, too. Oh they smiled and made a fuss of Jemima, certainly, but she had suddenly become very aware of her little-sister status. And that was going to last for the rest of her life. Not that she resented it. But . . .

'You are the best seer I have known,' Mrs Veroomes told Jemima firmly. 'Your ability is without equal. Your gift is just as great as that of your sister. I will help you polish it, never fear.'

'I know,' Jemima said glumly. 'But she's the one they all want. Oh, I know I'm being unfair.'

'They have started asking for you, too, Princess,' Felix said, his tail standing straight. 'Your father has arranged many appointments for later this afternoon.'

'Yeah – to pat me on the head or give me another gold necklace.' Not that she didn't like all the presents –

although Dad had forbidden her to take any back to the Outer Realm.

Felix and Mrs Veroomes exchanged a puzzled glance.

'The countryside folk need you desperately now the Karraks' false winter is lifting,' Felix said.

Jemima frowned. 'What? Why?' She adored Felix, but he could be really annoying at times.

'You are the Blossom Princess, Jemima.'

'Yeah, I know that.'

Felix chattered his teeth again. 'In this realm, titles are given for a reason.' His paw gripped her arm, and he gently turned her round. 'Look,' he said, gesturing. 'Look where you have walked.'

Jemima's breath caught in her throat. The winding path she'd taken through the palace gardens was now dusted with colour. Leaf buds were shining green on the branches of the empty trees. Flutterseeds were opening on the twigs of the bushes, their petals beginning to flap. Wildflower stalks were pushing up out of the ground's icy crust. 'Did I do that?' she gasped.

'Yes,' Felix said. 'It is your blessing to bring colour and life wherever you go. And with that comes hope and happiness. Always.'

27

HOME TO MUM

Dino Paganuzzi's ancient green Land Rover turned into the prim, brick-paved drive, and he grated his way up a gear.

Taggie resisted rolling her eyes heavenward. Her father had spent over fifty years in the Outer Realm, but he'd still not got the hang of gears. Another squeal of anguished metal, making her wince, and they came to a halt in front of Mum's house. It was an ultra-modern new-build in a village just outside of Stamford, with solar panels on the roof and half the walls made out of glass. A little automatic mower edged slowly along the front lawn.

Taggie had hated saying goodbye to the First Realm and all the friends she'd made there, even though Dad assured her that she would only be away while she was at school. 'You will return – it is your duty and destiny,' he promised. He would sit on the shell throne in her absence, until she finished school and grew up.

'But I can visit in the holidays,' she persisted.

'You will be *required* to visit in the holidays,' he assured her.

So yes, it was awful coming back. But seeing Mum's

house brought a small lump to her throat. It meant her life would be calm and ordinary for a while. Which, she was beginning to realize, was no bad thing either.

Jemima was first out of the Land Rover. She sprinted round to the back of the house and slid the big glass door open. The kitchen inside was perfectly neat, with every work surface polished to a gleam, and all Mum's amazing cooking gadgets in their proper place. 'Mum, we're home,' Jemima yelled. She thought she heard Mum moving around upstairs.

A big silver-edged card on the mantelpiece caught her eye. She went over and took it down, reading with growing excitement.

THE CHIEF EQUERRY TO

HER MAJESTY QUEEN ELIZABETH II

CORDIALLY REQUESTS THE PLEASURE OF

MISS AGATHA PAGANUZZI

AND

MISS JEMIMA PAGANUZZI

FOR TEA AT BUCKINGHAM PALACE

Jemima's eye shone with wonder. 'She remembered!' And wasn't Taggie going to be so cross when she saw her actual name written on the invitation! Jemima giggled in delight.

There was a soft rustling sound behind her and she turned round . . .

*

Taggie carried two of her bags, while Dad sagged under the weight of all the others.

'Did Jemima bring some of her gifts back?' he grumbled. 'These certainly feel like they're stuffed with gold.'

'No, Dad,' Taggie said, hoping he didn't spot the necklace she was wearing. But it had come from Earl Maril'bo – the pendant was a spark of starlight from the Fifth Realm, he'd told her when he'd given it to her. No way was she leaving that behind. And the same went for the friendship braid of bright red hair from Sophie that was currently swishing gently round her right ankle. Thankfully Dad agreed that she could wear the charmsward in the Outer Realm. 'Just in case,' as he put it. 'It's not just the denizens of the Dark Universe that are dangerous these days.'

'This is a nice garden,' Felix said as he bounded along at their feet. 'I think I'll enjoy camping here.'

'I'll open the window so you can get into my room,' Taggie assured him.

'That's very kind, Majesty, but I promised the Blossom Princess I'd sleep in *her* room.'

'Oh,' Taggie said, only slightly put out. 'OK then.'

'You can look after yourself,' Dad said. 'I'll be happier with Felix keeping an eye on Jem.'

'Sure,' Taggie said as they went round the corner of the house on to the patio. 'Seriously, though – how are we going to explain what happened to Mum? I didn't phone her once. She'll be so cross.'

265

'Leave your mother to me,' Dad said.

'Well, all right,' she said, and shoved the kitchen door open with her elbow. 'That's nice, but I'm the one who'll have to—' She jumped in shock.

Jemima was standing perfectly still at the far end of the kitchen. Lord Golzoth stood behind her, holding a glowing violet blade to her throat.

'One word,' he hissed through his silver-tipped teeth, 'and I slit her throat. If any of you move, I slit her throat. If I see that diabolical bracelet begin to turn, I slit her throat. Do you understand?'

Taggie nodded. She could see the fear and misery in Jem's eyes. It was all she could do not to rush over to her sister.

'You . . .' Golzoth growled dangerously. 'Weldowen skunk. Don't think I don't see you skulking about down there. Get up where you're in full view.'

Felix hopped up on to the kitchen's shiny marble work surface, his little black eyes glaring at the Karrak Lord.

'What do you want?' Dad asked calmly.

Taggie heard someone coming down the stairs. Her gaze flicked to the door to the hall. There must be something she could do to stop Mum coming in. But she knew how intently the devilsome Karrak was watching her.

'What do I want?' Golzoth asked. 'Your daughter slaughtered my brothers and sisters, and you ask what I want? My only sorrow is that I cannot extend your pain as I originally promised.'

'Really?' Dad said in a voice that was almost mocking. 'Look, you've still got time to get out. Be smart – forget all this, just walk away. That way, no one gets hurt.'

Lord Golzoth's teeth started to stretch out into silver fangs as he hissed in annoyance.

'Let Jem go,' Taggie blurted. 'Please. It's me you want.'

'Indeed I do,' Lord Golzoth said. 'And my dearest Queen of Dreams, making you watch your family die in front of you will be no small gratification for me. One I intend to fully enjoy. Almost as much as I will enjoy *your* death. Ah, now who is this come to join us?'

'Don't do it,' Dad urged.

The door handle turned, and Taggie watched helplessly as her mother walked into the kitchen. Mum stopped abruptly and looked at the Karrak Lord in his swirling smoke cloak the way she stared at their cat whenever it left muddy paw prints across her clean floor. 'What is going on here?' she demanded. 'Who are you?'

The Karrak Lord laughed. 'I am death,' he snarled, and brought his arm round and up, to point his long, bone fingers at Mum.

'No!' Taggie screamed.

The Karrak Lord's blue death spell spat across the room. Taggie watched in horror, unable to do a single thing to stop it. But the flare of deathly wizard light crunched to a halt centimetres from her mother. And suddenly Mum wasn't dressed in a pretty summer dress and pink cardigan any more. She wore imperious robes with a jewelled collar

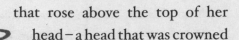

that rose above the top of her head – a head that was crowned in a tiara carved from a single diamond. Taggie thought she looked utterly breathtaking.

The death spell withered away.

Lord Golzoth managed to grunt: 'Oh.'

And Mum was just Mum again. 'Go away,' she said. And clicked her fingers.

There was a flash of darkness, sucking all the light out of the kitchen. Taggie blinked. There was no Lord Golzoth any more. Instead, soft twinkling ash was drifting down everywhere. All Taggie could think was how cross Mum would be about so much dirt messing up her precious kitchen.

Dad winced. 'I did try and tell you,' he said to the thin sparkly cloud which was now all that remained of the Karrak Lord.

Felix's teeth were chittering in astonishment. 'A Third Realm sorceress!' he gasped. 'Your mother is a Third Realm sorceress? When were you going to tell me *that*?'

Jemima let out a yelp, and ran across the room to Mum, who folded her arms around her. 'There, there, darling. It's all right, that dreadful buffoon won't be annoying anyone again.'

Taggie was so stunned she simply couldn't move.

Mum smiled reassuringly at her. 'Now then, young lady, I think you'd better tell me what you've all been up to. Start at the beginning, and don't leave anything out.'

THE END . . .

. . . of *The Secret Throne*. What happens next to Taggie, Jemima, Felix and Sophie will be told in *The Hunting of the Princes*, the second book in The Queen of Dreams trilogy.

ACKNOWLEDGEMENTS

My thanks to St Ives Surf School (www. stivessurfschool.co.uk) for their patience teaching me the basics of surfing. Any mistakes made converting their solid techniques to the way Earl Maril'bo goes boarding are all mine.

Peter F. Hamilton

Read an exclusive extract from

The Hunting of the Princes

Book two in Peter F. Hamilton's

The Queen of Dreams trilogy

Coming in summer 2016

1

A QUIET RIDE HOME

Taggie Paganuzzi was cycling home when her mobile rang. It was a four-mile ride from Stamford back to her mum's house. The tiny country road just outside the lovely old market town cut a winding route past fields guarded by ancient stone walls. Nobody else was using it.

Today was a warm sunny day, and now Taggie was thirteen her Mum was quite relaxed about her being out on her own. It probably helped that Mum was a Third Realm sorceress and Taggie had inherited that side of the family's magical strength. So while a lot of parents these days were fussy about allowing their daughters out by themselves, getting permission to go swimming at the municipal pool with her school friends was no problem for Taggie.

The mobile kept on ringing with the annoying tune she'd deliberately chosen for her younger sister, Jemima. It was the only sound she could hear. Taggie squeezed the brake and came to a halt beside one of the big oak trees lining the narrow road.

There was the faint noise of an engine in the distance as Taggie took off her backpack and started rummaging through it for the mobile. Her charmsward bracelet caught on the bag's big zipper. The charmsward was made up with several slim bands of brass and wood that were twined together. They were engraved with symbols which even after a year of wearing it Taggie wasn't completely familiar with. But it was what the charmsward contained that was truly important, the memories of all Taggie's First Realm ancestors who'd sat on the shell throne. It was like having a dictionary of spells permanently in her head.

Finally she pulled her mobile out of the bag, disentangling it from the wet towel. The sound of the engine was growing louder now. Taggie looked over her shoulder to catch a glimpse of a huge black motorbike slicing along the road towards her. The small rider was dressed in black leather with a matching shiny black helmet.

She tapped the 'accept call' icon.

'Death Spell!' Jemima's voice yelled out of the mobile. 'Duck!'

Taggie looked up, her mouth opening to grunt: 'Uh?' The motorbike was twenty yards away, rushing headlong at her with incredible speed, its rider sitting up in the saddle, an arm raised high with deadly blue magical light flaring around each finger.

Taggie instinctively shoved her own arm out towards the black rider. The charmsward bands spun smoothly, their slender engravings shining violet as the wave symbol lined up with the moonstar and a shield. '*Elakus!*' Taggie bellowed, and felt the shielding enchantment coil protectively around her.

A vivid-blue death spell flashed out from the rider's hand like a hostile comet. It hit Taggie's enchantment shield. The impact was like being struck by the boulder at the front of an avalanche. Taggie was knocked off the bike's saddle to flail about in mid-air before crashing painfully on the shaggy grass verge. But the shield enchantment held and the death spell sizzled down into the ground, killing the grass as it went.

Taggie was badly frightened and she was in a lot of pain. And she was incredibly angry that someone should just

273

come along and try to murder her like this. Even before she hit the verge the charmsward bands were sliding round again, aligning rock with wind. She landed on her side, skidding along through grass, nettles and brambles. Her hand pointed a rigid forefinger at the back of the rider who had zipped past. '*Israth hyburon*,' she growled furiously, and her arm lit up like a neon orange sign. The hot summer air in front of her warped as if she was looking through a giant magnifying glass. It became a big translucent fist that surged forward. The motorbike was punched up into the air, its engine shrieking wildly, wheels spinning. And the rider went flying over the drystone wall, legs and arms waving frantically.

The motorbike thumped down, banging and scraping along the tarmac until it finally came to a halt and its noisy engine stalled. Silence reclaimed the country lane.

Taggie staggered to her feet, wincing at the sharp pain in her bleeding knee. Now the shock was fading she realized how strong that death spell had been; even Jothran, the Karrak Lord who had tried to steal the shell throne from her last year, hadn't been this powerful. 'So who in all the heavens is the rider?' she asked herself with growing worry. Her instinct was to get back on her bicycle and get away as fast as she could, as the idea of fighting some crazed killer was terrifying. But she suspected attempting to flee wouldn't be any use. This had to be faced down.

She was shaking with fright as she refreshed the shield enchantment. Then it was a slow limp towards the moss-covered wall where the rider had gone over. By the time Taggie reached it, she was in no mood to waste time clambering over.

'*Droiak!*'

A wide section of wall exploded as her destruction spell hit it, sending smoking chunks of stone shooting up into the air. Mum and Dad were always telling her not to use magic here in the Outer Realm, but right now she decided normal rules didn't apply. Besides, technically she was a Queen, so she could do whatever she liked – although that never seemed to count for as much as you'd think with either parent.

Taggie stepped through the gap, and looked around for her assailant. But there was no sign of the black-clad rider. The meadow spread out ahead of her, with a flock of very startled sheep staring at her. There was nowhere for anyone to hide. 'What? How—'

Another death spell came streaking down out of the sky, hitting Taggie's shield right in front of her face with a fizzing burst of brilliant blue light. Again she went tumbling backwards, smacking into the remnants of the wall. 'Oww!' she cried. Her hand automatically went to her stinging nose. When she took it away there was blood on her fingers. The sheep were running away as fast as their spindly legs could manage.

Above her a huge black eagle swooped round in a fast curve.

A *shapeshifter*! Taggie realized in alarm. This was an incredibly complex magic that she'd never even tried to master. Anger finally overcame her fear. She stood up and snarled as she faced the eagle, which was soaring round to line up on her.

'OK then,' Taggie snapped. 'If that's the way you want it.' She hadn't asked for this battle, but if someone was stupid enough to try and kill a Paganuzzi with an unprovoked attack, they were going to have to learn the hard way what a seriously bad idea that was. Taggie licked her lips in determination as the charmsward's bands slid round obediently.

The eagle began its dive. Magic crackled around its talons.

'*Ti-Hath*,' Taggie chanted. Halfway between her and the eagle a wide circle of air turned rock hard.

The eagle smacked right into the patch of enchanted air at considerable speed. Its head crunched to one side, the rest of its body and wings followed, whacking into the solid sheet of air with equal force. 'Urrgh!' a girl's voice exclaimed. And for an instant the eagle was spread out wide in mid-air.

The dark bird slid vertically down the invisible barrier to the ground and flopped about on the meadow grass. A couple of feathers drifted down gently above it.

Taggie pointed her finger at the befuddled bird. '*Quillazen.*' A general counter-charm – that really ought to work on a shapeshift spell . . .

It did. The eagle shimmered, turning to a ball of seething black mist. And for a moment Taggie thought she was going to see a Karrak Lord emerge, the effect was so similar to the smoke cloaks they always wore to protect themselves from any kind of light.

Instead, a girl of about seventeen was revealed, wearing the black biker leathers. She was short and slender, with skin a shade darker than Taggie's, but with hair exactly the same rich chestnut. The nose was slightly flattened and the lips were thin. But it was the intense brown eyes that startled Taggie. It was like looking into a mirror.

The girl wiped a hand across her mouth, staring harshly at Taggie. 'You stupid little brat, you're ruining my reputation,' she said haughtily.

'Reputation?' Taggie's hand was still pointing warily at the girl, charmsward bands locked for another destruction spell. Taggie had never actually used a death spell but she was starting to think today might just be the day.

'I always kill quickly and cleanly and leave no sign of my presence.' The girl gestured angrily at the smoking stone wall. 'Now look!'

'Yeah, I'm really sorry about that,' Taggie said sarcastically.

The girl took a step closer, her back arching as if she was about to crouch then pounce. Taggie wished she'd just try it. Two years of martial arts lessons with Mr Koimosi, her sensei, had taught her a lot about physical combat. Especially when it came to brash arrogant people who thought they were superior because of their size and strength.

'Who are you?' she asked.

'The last person you'll ever see.'

'Oh dear. Did it take you a long time to come up with that? Or was it out of a Christmas cracker?' Taggie retorted.

The girl snarled. She clicked her fingers and another death spell came flashing out of her hand. It broke apart on Taggie's shield. Taggie flung her destruction spell, which the girl parried. Magical light flared and danced through the air between them. As it cleared, Taggie screamed. A massive snake was hurtling towards her. Taggie hated snakes. She stumbled backwards squealing in fright, but the snake just kept coming. Its head was as big as hers, while the sinuous body with its black and livid-green scales was thicker than her leg. Jaws parted wide to reveal fangs as long as fingers, while a nasty forked tongue flicked out amid a piercing hiss.

The snake lunged forward. Taggie jumped back and collided with the big oak tree on the side of the road. Before she realized what was happening, the snake coiled around her and the oak trunk, binding her to the tree, pinning her arms at her side. Her enchantment shielding prevented the snake's scales from actually touching her, but the thick coil contracted, squeezing tight. Little purple cracks spread across the shielding. Taggie groaned at the pressure. She could barely breathe.

The snake looped a second coil of itself around her and the tree. Another patch of her enchantment shielding creaked as the purple stress-lines multiplied. Now most of Taggie's chest was a mass of slender glowing purple streaks.

Slowly the snake's head rose up in front of Taggie. The horrible tongue vibrated out between the fangs, which dripped gooey venom from their tips.

'They warned me you were strong,' the girl's voice said. 'But even so, you're hardly a match for someone with my superior skill.'

Taggie didn't dare try to channel any magic into an aggressive spell. It was taking all her strength to keep her enchantment shielding in place. And that was gradually failing under the terrible pressure the snake was applying. She looked round desperately for something that could help.

The snake's head snapped forward, trying to close its jaws around Taggie's neck. It was only just repelled by the enchantment shield. Purple light rained across Taggie's face.

Taggie caught sight of something moving through the meadow. It gave her an idea. One which was stupid, a completely mad idea. But she hadn't got anything else. '*Cozal-wo.*' She sent out a tiny courage enchantment that needed hardly any magic to make it work.

The snake's head withdrew, its red and green eyes studying her in puzzlement. 'So, you need bravery to face your doom?' the girl's voice sneered. 'Fancy having to use magic to give that to yourself.'

Taggie sucked down a breath. 'Yes. I don't suppose you need anything to reinforce your cowardice.' She was looking behind the snake's head to the meadow, where the ram from the flock of sheep began to run towards them. It was a big animal, with dirty-yellow horns curling up from its head.

The snake hissed angrily and its head snapped forward again. Taggie thought her shield would fail this time, but it held against the hammer blow. Just. Only a couple more strikes like that would break it now.

'I am no coward,' the girl claimed. 'My profession is among the most noble in all the Realms.'

'What Realm calls 'thug' a profession?'

As Taggie expected, her provocation made the snake pull its head back, ready to strike again. The jaws opened wide and the enraged hiss began. The hiss abruptly changed to an astounded wail of surprise and pain. The snake's huge head twisted round, and Taggie felt its body turn rigid with shock. The ram's horns had stabbed it, and Taggie was abruptly surrounded by writhing black mist again. Then she found herself face to face with the girl who was hugging her and the tree. She had an expression of wide-eyed suffering. The ram backed away, withdrawing his curving horns from the girl's bottom.

Taggie didn't waste time forming a spell. She headbutted the girl. *Hard*. Never mind how unregal that was.

Her assailant tottered back, letting out another anguished wail. Taggie held out her arm. It was tempting, but today wasn't going to be the day for a death spell after all. '*Israth hyburon*.'

Magical orange light flared once again. The air warped as it smashed forward, and the girl went somersaulting backwards to thud down on the road.

'Who *are* you?' Taggie demanded, closing in on the prone figure in black leathers. 'Who sent you?'

The girl growled wordlessly at her. Then with an impressively fast motion she sprang back to her feet like a gymnast coming out of a difficult manoeuvre. She looked over Taggie's shoulder and pressed her lips together in annoyance. 'Still need Mummy's help, do we? What a Queen you make.'

'I . . . what?'

The girl's hand made an impatient gesture, and the big black motorbike lifted itself upright. The engine burst into life, and she leaped on to its saddle.

'Hey!' Taggie yelled. Some part of her was desperate to know who she was dealing with, but an altogether more sensible part was extremely glad the terrible girl was leaving.

'Don't worry, I'll see you soon enough, Queen of Dreams,' the girl sneered, and twisted the throttle.

'Not if I see you first,' Taggie shouted in a shaky voice. It was a good comeback, but she didn't think the girl would hear her above the engine roar. And anyway she was already riding off, speeding away down the lane.